MAGGIE & The ORANGUTANS

MAGGIE & The ORANGUTANS

Nicolas FSZ

ISBN 978-3-9827029-1-9

www.maggiesadventures.com

Book Series

www.maggiesadventures.com

Maggie's Adventures

Maggie and The Orangutans

Coming Soon

Maggie in The Himalayas

Adventures in Progress

Maggie and The Nile Crocodile

Maggie in The Galapagos

Maggie and The Super Tusker

Maggie in The Amazon Rainforest

Maggie and The Bengal Tiger

Maggie Explores Point Nemo

Table of Contents

The Adventure Team

Jasmin (Adventurous wife)
Magalie (Inspiring daughter)
Charlie (Loving son)
Amanda (1st draft reader-editor-supporter)
Thomas Mc Brien (Developmental Editor)
James Anders Banks (Copy Editor)
Marta Dec (Layout designer)
Kim Sponaugle (Cover illustrator)
Mylène Séguy (Interior illustrator)
My parents (True believers and supporters)
Proofreaders (Amanda, Thomas, James, Clare, Diana)

Creating the first of many middle grade adventure books has been an incredible journey. I am deeply grateful to everyone who has supported me along the way. Your encouragement, insights, and unwavering belief in this project have been a blessing.

To my family, friends, and mentors; thank you for standing by my side, offering guidance, and cheering me on as Maggie's story came to life. Your love and support have been my compass throughout this adventure.

I am thrilled to continue this journey with you as Maggie embarks on her next thrilling adventure in The Himalayas, the second book in the *Maggie's Adventures* series. Here's to many more adventures ahead.

Nicolas FSZ.

N
O
E
S

Maggie's Adventures

Prologue

Our Home

Life thrives in our ever evolving environment we call home. With an estimated two million described species inhabiting planet Earth, researchers around the world have organised them into the following ten groups:

- Corals
- Mammals
- Amphibians
- Birds
- Reptiles
- Fishes
- Crustaceans
- Arachnids
- Molluscs
- Insects

We are all different in our own ways but have one thing in common:

OUR HOME

Planet Earth's ecosystem has been changing and evolving since the beginning of time, and we have, and will always need, heroes that work hard to do what they can to help sustain its beauty.

Maggie and her family are some of these heroes and, little does she know, she will play a crucial role in uniting us all.

Maggie was born on a warm summer's morning with the sound of birds chirping and the leaves rustling in the wind. Now an 11-year-old girl, full of energy and curiosity, she loves to be surrounded by nature and is always searching for wildlife wherever she goes. She is agile, strong, and very independent. She reads and listens to her elders' wisdom to understand the new environments she travels to and is always keen to learn more.

Since day one, she has travelled to some of the most remote regions of the world by her parents' side. Mama is a political environmentalist, and Papa is a professional outdoors photographer with a secret operative's past. They work hard to create a peaceful coexistence with the locals.

Maggie is always going on extraordinary adventures, meeting new friends, and gaining new skills along the way. Maggie finds her strength and power internally, studies hard to understand the various environments she lives in and brings her bravery and wits to the table when needed.

She lives amidst dense jungles, up on the highest peaks, far away on the world's oceans, deep into tropical forests and right by oasis riverbeds. Each quite different from the last, with one similar standpoint: most of these places need her help to restore balance to their natural beauty.

With the help from her new friends, her parents and her newly acquired skills, she plans out a way to help restore the natural order.

Chapter 1

The Arrival

A large wave smashed against the hull of The Jolly Roger and woke Maggie from her slumber. She lay awake in her cabin, listening to the ocean splashing around as she thought of her next destination, the island of Borneo. It was the beginning of May and both she and her parents were moving there to research its unique ecosystem. Maggie slipped into her drysuit and her life jacket before climbing up on deck as the sun rose over the horizon.

"Ahoy, matey," yelled Abrah. "What ye doin' up so urly?"

Abrah was The Jolly Roger's first mate, Maggie's good friend and favourite life guide. She looked around, still sleepy from her short night, and simply smiled. She walked over to the helm to stand next to Abrah.

That was when she saw it. Amidst the morning ocean mist, the island of Borneo made its first appearance. Her new home awaited their arrival. She could not hold herself back and hailed at the top of her voice.

"Land Ahoy!!" she bellowed.

"Arrg hahahaha!" Abrah burst out laughing as he picked Maggie up onto his shoulders.

The crew wearily started popping their heads out on deck to see for themselves the marvels of the coming island.

The Jolly Roger sailed into the bay ever so calmly. As it came into port, the crew spent the morning securing the sailboat's berth. Maggie, however, had other plans. As soon as they had secured the first heaving line, she was off discovering and meeting the local villagers. Before morning's end, she was surrounded by most of the local kids running and playing with her. She showed them around The Jolly Roger while her parents met the village chiefs to secure their new home and local presence.

The village chieftain showed them to some rafts and a group of villagers clambered aboard. Maggie and her parents were bustled into a larger raft with their local guide Zikri.

"We will take you to your new home now, we named it the Bamboo Nest. Sit in the centre and try not to rock the boat. Be aware of the crocodile lurking beneath the water's surface," Zikri said sternly, with a smile.

Maggie stayed very still in the centre of the raft. They rowed with the current along the rivers through the dense jungle. The occasional loud cawing, the constant rustling of leaves mixed with the buzzing insects seemed so familiar to Maggie's ears, even though she had never seen anything like it. As Zikri navigated them into a tunnel of trees, the calls of the wild dimmed. Everywhere Maggie looked, vines engulfed them. It was beautiful, with so many shades of green, yellow, and red, and when they could see it, the bluest sky above. The water was greenish brown like any jungle river. The three of them were in awe of their new home.

A couple of hours later, the group of rafts took a sharp turn into the tiniest waterway. They slid through the branches, under some fallen tree trunks and cut through some vines that blocked the way.

"We will arrive soon," Zikri said.

A few minutes later, they rowed into a clearing. Maggie looked up as the canopy opened above them. Up high by the treetops, she saw a magnificent house made entirely of bamboo, two storks stood on the banister overlooking the lagoon. The humid air was not as heavy on Maggie's cheeks, and the smell of exotic fruits filled her nostrils. She noted all the fruit trees surrounding her new home.

They rowed forwards to a jetty which led to a pathway towards their house and right up to the fruit trees. It was all linked to the balcony that circled the house and came back down to the water.

"The safety gates, bridges and lifts are set up to protect you. Please remain alert when you come down the pathway to the waterway and the jungle floor," Zikri said, looking directly at Maggie.

Chapter 2

The Bamboo Nest

Maggie leaped off the raft onto the pontoon, jumping over the gate with ease. She sprinted up the pathway to her Bamboo Nest, her footsteps echoing softly as the bamboo poles creaked beneath her. She instantly fell in love with her Bornean jungle home. Holding onto the balcony banister, she gazed into the surrounding jungle. The thick, vibrant greenery seemed to pulse with life, promising untold adventures just beyond her doorstep.

"Look over there!" she shrieked as she darted round the pathway, her eyes wide with excitement. Her heart pounded as she ran, but just as quickly as it had appeared, the creature she had seen melted back into the jungle, its fur a fleeting blur amongst the light brown branches.

"If you want to have a better look at the wildlife, you'll have to be more discreet. Blend into your surroundings, just as they do," Zikri advised Maggie with a chuckle.

The villagers helped bring all the luggage and gear up to the balcony and then went back to the village. Zikri stayed behind to help with the settling in. He prepared a nice local meal for their first night in Borneo. They all sat around the kitchen table for supper as darkness surrounded the house. The daytime cawing had ceased and was replaced by the occasional distant roar or nearby hooting.

Zikri leaned in, his voice low and deliberate. “Let me tell you a mystical story I was once told as a little boy.” His eyes flickered with something unreadable, the flickering candlelight casting shadows on his face. “Legend tells of an ancient hundred-foot slithering serpent which roams Borneo with eyes like burning embers.” He paused, letting the weight of his words settle. “Some believe it can shift form, to blend into its surroundings perfectly. Locals call it Nabau and believe it to be the guardian of the forest and rivers. They say when it dies, its body turns to stone, blending into the landscape.” He glanced over to Maggie, his voice a soft warning. “Explorers such as yourselves have found remains of strange, twisted rock formations up in Sarawak along the Rajang River. Locals swear they are the remains of Nabau lying still but not forgotten.”

Maggie’s brilliant mind went back to her book about Borneo’s legendary python Nabau, protector of the jungle and all its inhabitants.

“The Legendary Nabau. The python goddess of Borneo. Feared and revered by all of Borneo’s locals for centuries, even millennia. A myth for some, a true legend for others.” She quoted her book word for word.

“I see you have done some reading,” Zikri said proudly. “If you are lucky, the jungle will place its trust in you and you will meet Nabau, Goddess of the jungles and rivers," he continued mysteriously.

Over time, Maggie mastered the art of blending in. Thanks to her newly acquired skill, she spotted exotic birds, amphibians, so many arachnids, too many molluscs to count, and a few reptiles hanging from trees or scurrying back towards the water. She had not seen any crocodiles like Zikri mentioned but she was lucky enough to notice an elephant making its way through the jungle. She spotted a few mammals too, from white-bearded gibbons to a family of black-crested Sumatran langurs among others.

Maggie wanted to see all the animals living in the jungle of Borneo and she had seen a lot, but what she longed to see were the world-famous orangutans.

That morning, like most of her mornings in Borneo, she woke up to a feast of freshly picked fruits. She mixed them with a few dried cereals they had brought back from the village.

Before heading out on her daily adventure, Maggie knew she needed to finish her homework. She took her books and computer out and started reading her emails. Her tutors contacted her this way and provided her with her lessons. She was a bright girl and could do it all before lunch. This left her with the rest of the day to go exploring and do her own research and discoveries.

Before setting off, she double checked her backpack to make sure she had everything she needed. Over the months, her parents had taken Maggie on adventures, where they learnt everything there was to know about the risks and dangers of jungle life. Maggie's parents trusted her to be reasonable and safe with all the decisions that she took.

Maggie pulled out her map and compass, squinting at the markings as she oriented herself. She peered down at the lagoon, scanning the still water for any lurking crocodile or any other dangers before setting off. Beads of sweat trickled down her forehead pooling at the tip of her nose. The heavy, humid air wrapped around her like a wet blanket, making each step more ponderous than the last.

Her energy levels lifted when the scent of the most vibrant mangos and other exotic fruits filled the air. She paused for a second to pick fresh ones for the road. She was on her way again when her eyes fixed on some beautiful pink fruit trees just up ahead. She had never seen this fruit before. She was happy to put her backpack down to take the time to investigate her new find. She snapped a quick photo, intending to look it up later, and gently picked one from the tree. As she held this oval, egg-shaped, bright pink fruit, about the size of a large tennis ball, she realised how soft and leathery it felt in the palm of her hand. Caution tugged at her, reminding her that this beautiful fruit might be poisonous or require special preparation.

With her photos taken, and the fruit nestled safely in her backpack, Maggie set off again. As she walked southeast through the lush jungle, she stumbled upon a colossal Banyan tree, its massive trunk twisting and sprawling in all directions. Curiosity piqued, she approached cautiously, drawn to its dark hollow base.

Peering inside, she wrinkled her nose at the earthy scent of damp fungi and decay. The air was cool, a stark contrast to the warmth outside. Maggie looked up and could barely see the blue sky, and almost no direct sunlight seeped through the dense jungle canopy. She recalled reading about the Banyan tree's unique way of thriving in such a competitive environment. How it slowly enveloped a fully grown tree, using it as a scaffold to rise tall and strong, leaving a hollow interior as it drained the energy from its host. A sense of awe washed over her as she stood before this living testament to nature's intricate dance of survival.

She went a little further, hoping to run into some wildlife. She pushed her way past the overgrown vines, slashing away with her machete. Sweat was dripping down her forehead into her eyes. The saltiness made her eyes sting a little. As she moved forwards creating herself a path, she felt the jungle awaken around her. She heard the fluttering of a hundred birds flying off into the sky. The thunderous flapping was followed by the eeriest silence. Maggie was mesmerised by this sudden burst of energy filling her ears. This feeling was cut short by the rustling leaves and cracking of the branches nearby, sending a shiver down her spine. Her prudent instincts kicked in, and she quickly and quietly found her way back to the Banyan tree and hid inside its hollow trunk. She easily fit inside and had space for her backpack too. The moist smell of fungus engulfed her mouth and nose, and she could see creepy crawlies moving about the bark a few centimetres away from her face.

She turned to face the open crack, away from all the arachnids, myriapods and insects. From here, she peered out and saw trees bending and swinging in the distance. Something big was out there and heading directly towards her. A mixture of feelings engulfed her mind and body. She was fearful, excited, and curious all at once. In that moment, the inhabitants of the Banyan tree were the least of her problems.

Chapter 3

Dark and Menacing

Maggie's hands were trembling as fear engulfed her entire body. She wanted to flee in the opposite direction. She peered out from her hiding place and heard leaves rustling and branches cracking close by. She mustered all her bravery and remained hidden, becoming one with the hollow Banyan tree. She closed her eyes, concentrating on her breathing. In, out, feeling her abdomen move out with each inhalation and in again with every exhalation. Focusing on her breathing helped calm her heartbeat down to a gentle rhythmic lup-dup.

She opened her eyes. Silent and still, she scanned the jungle canvas. An immense orange figure elegantly swung into view, moving majestically from treetop to treetop, making entire trunks bend to its will. It was truly massive! Maggie's fear was replaced with excitement. She held onto the sides of the Banyan trunk, leaning out. Creepy crawlies were moving freely over her hands, but she did not mind the tickling sensation. Her dream encounter was happening. Her entire focus was on the massive orangutan effortlessly swinging from tree to tree a few metres away. She could clearly see him now, including his huge throat sack which allowed him to bellow loudly across the treetops and his large cheek pads. She knew this was a massive alpha male just up there in the trees.

She heard more branches crack further in the distance and instinctively turned her head. Surprised to see an entire troop following the alpha male, as they usually roam alone, she stepped out from her hiding place. Maggie had dreamt of seeing wild orangutans since her arrival. The beauty of these beings, calmly swaying through the jungle tops, warmed her inner spirit. Both eyes wide open, not to miss a second of this magical moment. She longed to be up there with them. She quietly swung her camera up to her left eye and managed to get a couple of perfect shots.

Maggie was out in the open when a young male must have seen her. He swooped down to get a closer look at their observer. They both stared at each other for a moment. She was in awe of this magnificent animal. The young orangutan was hooting at Maggie, as if trying to communicate. The rest of the troop looked around but continued swaying forwards. Before she had time to react, the young orangutan swung back up into the trees and out of sight.

"Woah! That was amazing!" Maggie said to herself. "Mum is going to love everything about this encounter. And Papa is going to love the shots," Maggie said, glowing with energy.

As she flickered through the photos, something strange caught her attention behind one of the larger orangutans bending an entire tree. In the corner of the frame, a thick plume of black smoke curled ominously into the sky. Her pulse quickened, a chill racing through her veins as the reality hit her. Could this be a forest fire? It couldn't be, but the smoke was there, dark and menacing. Her eyes shifted to the orangutans, swinging directly towards it, their carefree movements seemingly oblivious to the potential threat. Her stomach tightened. What if they were moving towards danger? What if she was? Questions raced through her mind as the jungle, once alive with wonder, now felt heavy with a hidden threat.

Was it nothing, or was everything about to change?

Chapter 4

The Gift

Maggie had started walking in the same direction as the troop when, out of nowhere, the same young orangutan jumped down in front of her. He stood there, right in front of Maggie, hooting away and waving his long arms frantically.

The orangutan calmed down, reaching his long arm to Maggie, slowly unfolding his grip. Maggie noticed in the palm of his hairy hand the pink fruit she had seen earlier. This one was much smaller and was a lighter shade of pink than the one Maggie had picked. He handed it over to her quite abruptly, Maggie accepted the gift nonetheless, amazed by her new friend's actions. The moment she had it in her hands the orangutan showed her a second pink fruit. He ate it in a way suggesting Maggie should do the same. She was still sceptical of eating a new fruit without knowing what it was. She decided to go with her gut feeling and trust the young orangutan, and she took a bite.

This was one of the tastiest, most delicious fruit she had ever tasted. Sweet, mixed in with a slight tangy twist on her tastebuds. Her mouth was watering for another bite. Still in awe of her encounter, she wanted to capture this moment forever. As the orangutan was hooting away and blowing raspberries, Maggie brought her camera to her eye and started shooting portrait photos.

Maggie was ecstatic about her encounter and the opportunity she was getting to take such photos. A slight tingle rushed around her body, her feet feeling ever so light as if she were floating above the leafy jungle floor. That was when she realised her new friend's noises were starting to sound like words and audible sounds. She could understand the orangutan!

"What are you doing here?" the orangutan hooted.

Maggie was so taken aback, she had to pinch herself several times to make sure she was not dreaming.

"Can... Can you talk?" she asked hesitantly, questioning herself for talking to a wild animal.

"I can," he said very proudly. "My gift enabled you to understand me," he continued.

"This is spectacular! No one will ever believe me! Thank you for the fruit, it was the tastiest, most delicious fruit I have ever eaten."

"Don't mention it. We call it an Engkala. What are you doing here?" he asked.

"I moved to the jungle a few months ago with my parents, but right now I am on my daily adventure wandering through the jungle. I am Maggie, by the way. What is your name?" Maggie asked politely, remembering she was wandering through the orangutan's home.

"I am Drew. It is nice to meet you, Maggie, and I welcome you to the jungle of Borneo."

Maggie looked at Drew in awe. "It is nice to meet you, Drew. I have been dreaming of meeting an orangutan for so long now."

Drew looked at Maggie. He was as pleased to have met her as she was to have met him.

"Now that you have, would you care to join us for a wander through the jungle tops?" Drew asked Maggie, hoping to introduce his new friend to the leader of the troop.

Maggie was a little hesitant of climbing such tall trees, but realised this might be the only chance she would get to do so.

"Would I ever!" she exclaimed.

"Then jump up and follow me. We need to catch up with the others."

With those last words, Drew shot up into the trees.

"Trust your instincts. Use your hands to grip onto the largest vines you can hold and thrust your bodyweight into the direction you want to go," Maggie heard Drew yell.

She let her mind go free, spotted the vine she was going to grab and broke into a run. She gathered momentum and jumped, just as Drew had said. Before she knew it, she was swaying through the jungle's canopy, just like she had seen Drew and his family doing earlier. She could feel the strain in her arms. Her grip was so tight around the vines, her knuckles were white and her palms red. The wind was rushing through her hair. She had to plan her swings a couple of vines ahead if she was to keep a steady rhythm.

She had quickly caught up with the group of orangutans, who were still moving towards the black smoke she had noticed in her photograph. They all turned their heads to look at her. Maggie saw the large alpha male at the front of the troop, and he turned to Drew.

"Who is your new friend?" he bellowed, looking over his shoulder.

Drew looked over at Bosco and bowed his head.

"Her name is Maggie, she moved here a few months ago with her parents. Can she join us for the day?" Drew asked innocently.

"Only if she can keep up," the leader said, smiling at Maggie.

And off they went, swinging from branch to branch through the jungle heights, Maggie ecstatic to be living her dream.

Chapter 5

The Fruit Bonanza

Maggie and the troop arrived at a clearing and came to a halt. Maggie was getting hungrier by the minute, and the magical scent of juicy tropical fruits was making her mouth water and her stomach grumble. The scene turned into a fruit bonanza, and everyone was eating their fill. Bosco had navigated his troop to a fruit field.

Drew signalled Maggie to follow him as he lunged to a neighbouring mango tree. He tossed one to her as she found a nice vine to hang from.

"Try this one," he said with half a mango dripping out of his jaws.

As she peeled its skin back, Maggie could not help but think of the thick, black smoke rolling up into the sky from the heart of the jungle. She decided to mention it to Drew.

"Drew. Did you notice the black smoke rising from the heart of the jungle? I am worried we are closer to it than we would want to be," Maggie said. Her voice must have carried, as the others turned around anxiously.

"Yes, our leader Bosco knows about it. He also knows too well how dangerous such smoke is in our jungle," Drew said in a quiet tone.

Drew was called away by his mother. Maggie realised she had touched a soft spot, and it might be time to head home. She took her short-range radio out to call her parents and saw she had a missed call with a message.

"Maggie my dear, your Papa and I have just returned home. Please be on your way home before bedtime, the sun is on its way down. We love you, my dear. See you later."

She put her walkie-talkie away safely in her backpack. She stretched her right arm out to a close hanging vine and wrapped her fingers tightly as she let herself swing down using gravity. The leaves swished by gently around her as she approached Bosco.

"It is getting quite late, and the sun is coming down. Would it be possible to take me back home?" she asked politely.

Bosco looked down at her from his towering composure. "Of course. Just one more stop on the way and I will take you home myself," he bellowed softly.

The gang started to climb up instead of straight. They were going higher and higher. Higher than Maggie had ever been before. She could not even see the ground anymore and they were still climbing.

They were climbing to the top of the jungle where the most spectacular view was awaiting them. The contrast between the vibrant dark greens of the jungle canopy and the clear blue sky was out of this world. Fiery oranges were mixing into the flaming yellows and turning into reds as the sun was setting.

The troop settled down, the little ones snuggled up with their Mamas ready for sleep. Bosco grabbed hold of Maggie ever so gently and swung her onto his back.

"Get a good grip on my fur. I will take you home now," he said gently.

As she was tightening her grip, she spotted movement on the horizon. The dismal black smoke was flowing upwards out of the heart of the jungle. Bosco stopped to stare at it too.

"Smoke is always bad news in this jungle," he murmured sadly.

Chapter 6

A New Day

That night was filled with dreams of swinging through treetops and eating her fill of the juiciest fruits. When she woke up, she lay there with her eyes closed, trying to go back to her dreamland, her muscles still sore from yesterday's swinging and climbing. The rustling of leaves outside her window and her Mama's gentle humming meant fresh fruits for breakfast.

She made her way over to the kitchen to find her mother had already cleaned, trimmed, and sliced them up ready to be eaten. Maggie took a bowl out of the kitchen cupboard, threw in some oats and homemade yoghurt, topped it all off with the freshly picked fruits, and breakfast was served. As she ate, she could not help but be reminded of the pink Engkala Drew had given her.

Her mind wandered off as she recalled yesterday's adventure. She thought back to her orangutan friends and her heart started racing with excitement. She could still feel the wind brushing her face while she swung from vine to vine.

There was still so much to explore, and the ominous black smoke was on her mind. She was ready for a new jungle adventure. Jumping from her chair, she cleared up the kitchen and got ready for the day. No emails or schoolwork on Saturdays, she thought to herself with a smile. She saw her parents on the balcony and went to hug them goodbye before setting off. She was eager to go.

"I have my radio with me, and I will stay in range, I promise," Maggie told her Mama as she ran around the house to the other side to the pathway.

Maggie checked her surroundings, making sure the coast was clear amidst the leafy bottom. She was about to naturally walk down the pathway to the jungle floor when she smiled and grabbed hold of a large dangling vine. She let her instincts take over and started swinging just as Drew had shown her. She let out an enthusiastic cheer.

In the rush, she realised she had forgotten to pack her camping gear. Leaving without all the proper gear was not a safe way to start any adventure. She quickly went back home to pick up her hammock and mosquito net. Before swinging off her balcony once more, she quickly glanced at her compass and started heading east.

The branches bent with her weight, and the leaves rustled as she swung by at the end of the vines. She was moving through the jungle tops with ease, letting her mind wander off when she felt a cold shiver run down her spine. The memory of the black smoke and the worried look on Bosco's face were in the back of her mind. As she swung, her hand slipped. Her heart stopped as she fell through the air. Thump, she fell onto a large branch. She was losing her concentration and needed to focus her mind.

She moved on a little further and found a comfortable, safe place up in the trees where she could sit and let her mind relax. She had been taught that the power of the mind can be controlled through meditation, and she knew that was what she needed to do. She started to calm her breathing and heartbeat to focus her mind.

She sat on a huge branch, so wide she could easily sit cross-legged without having to worry about slipping over the edge.

Very softly and slowly, she breathed in, and then breathed out, breathed in, and then breathed out. She let her mind flow to the many jungle sounds, focusing on using her belly muscles to fill and empty her lungs. The insects' buzzing around the jungle air mixed into the birds' chirping from their nests as the trees creaked and leaves rustled. All the sounds mixed and became one in the background. She was beginning to be at one with her surroundings.

She'd learnt that meditation is the art of silencing one's mind by focusing on a recurring action. Maggie focused on her breathing, and whenever a thought came into her mind, she simply recognised it and let it go, by focusing her mind on her inhalation and her exhalation once again.

Her mind, empty and relaxed, drifting through the spiritual realm of meditation. Her breathing had calmed down, and her heartbeat had slowed to an even pace when the dark mystical black cloud slowly crept into her thoughts and frightened her into opening her eyes wide. In the blink of an eye, she relived the moment she saw the smoke rise high into the sky.

Then and there, she knew she needed to find out what it was, and help anyone it put in danger. She climbed to the highest branch of the tallest tree, peered her head out through the leaves and looked all around. Her heart sank when she saw that nothing but jungle surrounded her. Maggie felt overwhelmed by the size of the jungle. If only she could find her way back to the fruit field, she would know in which direction to head.

Chapter 7

A Campsite Like no Other

A soft sigh escaped her as the sun dipped lower, casting long shadows through the canopy. She glanced at the sky, biting her lip. Her eyes narrowed as she weighed her options. Home was about an hour away, but the jungle ahead beckoned her forward. Kneeling by her backpack on a large branch, she rummaged through it, fingers brushing against her familiar gear as she made sure she had everything she needed.

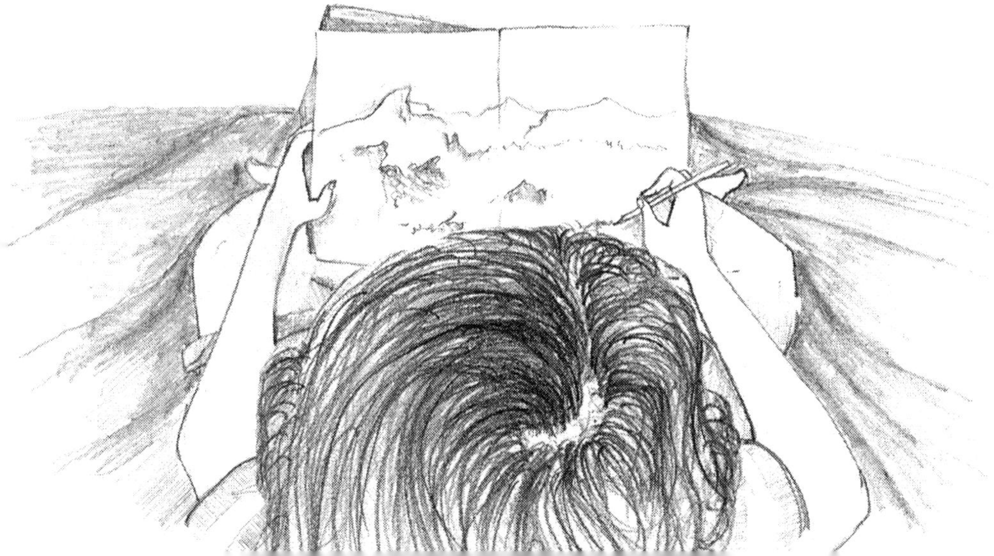

Gripping her radio, she brought it to her lips, her voice steady despite the growing darkness.

"Mama? Can I stay out tonight?" A pause, then a crackle of static. She waited, her hand tightening around the strap of her backpack.

After a moment, her mother's voice came through, faint but clear.

"Okay, but be back before dinner tomorrow."

Relief washed over her. Slinging her backpack over her shoulders, she continued onwards.

Swinging through the treetops, she inhaled deeply, the air rich with a light, sweet aroma. Guided by the enchanting scent, clenching her fists firmly around each new vine, she swung from tree to tree, enjoying the lush scenery and stopping from time to time to take a quick photo.

The sweet fragrance grew stronger, pulling her closer. Her heart raced as she spotted the first fruits peeking through the foliage, their colours vivid against the greenery. She celebrated her arrival by plucking one of each to savour their juicy aromas.

After devouring the fruits, she stretched her arms towards the canopy and climbed upwards until her fingertips brushed against the topmost branches. Above her, the sky unfurled, a deepening blue, as she scanned the horizon for any sign of the horrifying black smoke. Disappointment crept in as she found only wisps of light fog and the sun dipping low.

With a firm resolve, she chose a sturdy branch overlooking the jungle and began to set up camp. She raised her radio, her voice steady as she assured her parents she was safe.

Though Maggie had spent nights under the stars with her father and at times alone near home, nothing compared to this adventure. She secured her hammock high among the branches, sinking into its embrace while gazing over the sprawling jungle, the vibrant sunset painting the sky. What a life, she thought, a smile creeping across her face before she fell fast asleep.

She stirred at first light with the soft cooing birds and the rustling of the leaves and branches in the breeze. Blinking against the golden dawn, she propped herself up. The sunrise over the Bornean jungle exploded with colours that seemed to have leapt off the pages of her drawing books.

She fumbled for her camera, snapping a few quick photos, then pulled out her sketchbook and a set of vibrant colouring pencils. With each stroke, she tried to capture the magic unfolding around her. Deep blues melting into lush greens, then bright yellows tinged with fiery oranges and reds. The trees transformed under the sun's embrace, shifting from dark silhouettes to vibrant greens, their leaves glistening like jewels.

As she sketched, a sense of calm enveloped her. Each line etched the moment deeper into her memory, a beautiful reminder of this awe-inspiring morning.

Chapter 8

Breakfast with Friends

She heard branches cracking and saw the trees weaving from side to side. She lay in her hammock listening carefully, trying to pinpoint where the noise was coming from. Whatever was making the trees weave and crack was coming towards the fruit field just beneath her campsite. Maggie remained hidden up in her hammock, alert to any sound that would give away what was moving through the jungle down below. She reached her hand out to the vine above and started pulling her weight off her hammock so she could get a better look at what was down there. Drew jumped out from behind the thick foliage to her left.

"Aieeeeeee!" Maggie shrieked in fright as she fell back into her hammock.

Drew was laughing his fur off. Maggie clambered out onto the branch below, heart still racing from her friend's practical joke. She smiled at Drew and joined the troop for breakfast, first paying her respects to the elders. She made her way to Drew's father, Bosco. He greeted Maggie like his own and offered her a juicy half-opened papaya fruit. They sat there enjoying breakfast.

"You should try to be more aware of your surroundings, little one," Bosco said insightfully and with a chuckle.

He smiled at her and continued eating the half papaya. Maggie looked up at Bosco and smiled nervously.

"Bosco," Maggie started inquisitively. "My mind cannot stop thinking of the smoke we noticed the other night at sunset.

"Smoke is bad news for anything close by," he interrupted abruptly.

"I realise that," Maggie insisted. "I am worried about the safety of the jungle."

The alpha male stopped chewing his fruit. He remained silent and pensive.

"We orangutans move away from such things. We know smoke means trouble. Trouble often caused by humans."

His gaze went from alarmed to worried when he realised what she was going to ask next.

"Would you help me find the source of the smoke?" Maggie asked.

Bosco chuckled nervously at Maggie's audacity.

"Hehehe, you are asking a lot of my troop, little girl. We are heading south away from the smoke and its dangers. But I will divert my troop slightly to the east, so you get a bit closer to your goal."

He then swung down a few branches to get some more fruits. Maggie did not overstay her welcome and swung back to where Drew was sitting eating a fresh mango.

Drew had a worried look about him after hearing they were going to get closer to the smoke. It soon vanished when he saw a huge coconut hanging a few trees away.

Maggie had eaten her fill and was pondering about the cause of this potential fire. She was worried about the animals that could be hurt or trapped. She took out her map, figured out where she was, and marked it with a big pineapple and some notes.

Bosco made a loud grunting sound and headed off, his troop following closely behind. Maggie took a heading with her compass and followed suit with Drew.

They were getting close to the heart of the jungle when a peculiar smell surrounded them. All faces were pointed upwards, sniffing at the air, trying to identify what this smell might be. As the troop fell silent, they could hear the loud whacking sound of an axe as it bit into a thick trunk. A tree groaned and creaked loudly, its massive weight straining against the final cuts, followed by a deep, echoing crack, splitting the air as the tree snapped free. The ground trembled beneath a thunderous crash as the giant tree finally collapsed, shaking the jungle floor.

They all felt it and huddled up together up in the treetops ready to flee if needed. Bosco moved forwards to check it out. Maggie, Drew, and the other young ones were kept together, surrounded by the elders.

Bosco appeared, and he had a sad look on his face.

"We have to go," he said firmly. "We need to get away from this area and head as far south as we can."

He turned to Maggie. "Be careful what you are looking for, little girl. These humans are not your friends."

Before she had time to say anything, the troop headed south with a demoralised swing in each of their movements. Only one looked back to see Maggie fade away amongst the dense jungle bush.

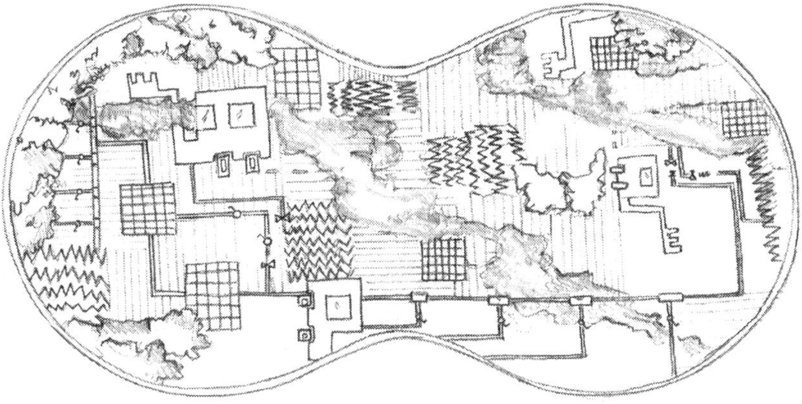

Chapter 9

The Worksite

Bosco's sudden departure gnawed at her, the urgency in his actions pulling her into motion. Without hesitation, she lowered herself onto the nearest branch, her body moving like a shadow through the thick canopy. Leaves brushed her face as she clung to the vines, still and silent.

The faint sound of movement in the distance reached her ears. Carefully, she slipped her hand into her backpack, her fingers wrapping around her binoculars. Lifting them to her eyes, she peered through the branches. Deep in the heart of the jungle, where no one should be, she spotted them. Humans and their towering machines glinting under the dappled sunlight, monstrous against the natural green of the forest. Her breath hitched. She had to get closer.

Maggie climbed higher, her hands gripping the bark as she slowly and quietly moved from tree to tree. Each motion swift and calculated, drawing her nearer to the workers.

Maggie slipped through the branches until she reached the edge of the quarry's clearing, her breath shallow as she pressed her body against the rough bark. The other humans were close now, too close. She remembered what Zikri had told her about blending in as she melted into the shadows, her skin prickling as she became part of the jungle. Still, silent, and watching. Her heart pounded, but her mind sharpened. She remembered the stories Abra would tell her, during the long ocean crossings, about illegal work camps, filled with dangerous, ruthless people. She had thought they were just that: stories. Every instinct told her to stay hidden.

Voices rose from below, sharp and urgent. She peered through the leaves. Men barked orders, words clipped and hard. Some hauled empty cages, the metal gleaming under the sun, large enough to hold a bear. Others operated the massive machines that roared through the forest, the earth beneath them shaking as trees splintered and fell, their destruction brutal and swift.

Then came the shrill, piercing clatter of a stork's bill. Its cry echoed through the chaos. The sound was so loud, so desperate, that Maggie flinched, her hands, instinctively flying up to cover her ears.

She glanced down and saw them. Two Storm's storks, rare and magnificent, being shoved into cages like lifeless cargo. The sight twisted something deep inside her. Anger! Horror! They couldn't do this!

Her hands trembled as she shoved the binoculars back into her bag. That was when she saw him, a man moving directly below her. His footsteps heavy, eyes scanning the treetops. Panic shot through her veins. She shifted to retreat, but her fingers fumbled. The binoculars slipped from her grasp, and THUD! The noise they made hitting the ground was impossibly loud. Maggie froze.

The man's head snapped up. His gaze locked onto the trees above him, his shout splitting the air as he pointed in Maggie's direction. His arm shot out as he scrambled for a better view, boots crushing the fallen leaves beneath him. Maggie's breath caught in her throat, fear surging through her chest. She didn't wait to see what would happen next. She sprang into motion, swinging upward into the safety of the canopy, disappearing into the dense green jungle before they could catch another glimpse of her.

Despite the terror gripping her chest, Maggie's eyes darted around, searching for safety. She spotted a thick branch, high above the chaos. She swung onto it, settling into the perfect vantage point where she could stay hidden, wrapped in the forest's protective green cocoon.

Her fingers trembled as she reached into her bag, pulling out her camera. Her heart raced, but her hands moved with purpose. She snapped picture after picture, the cages, the men, the machinery, trying to capture every inch of the worksite to bring back evidence of the destruction.

No wonder Bosco looked so saddened and had left so urgently.

It was time for Maggie to head home. It took Maggie a good hour to swing home, but with her resolve to help save the jungle from these monsters, it went by in a flash. Maggie saw her jungle home amidst the trees. Her parents were there, lovingly waiting for her. They saw Maggie swinging from tree to tree and were a bit taken aback. Maggie did not even think about it and just went straight to them and jumped into their arms from the treetops. She melted into tears. Maggie's parents were bewildered but they just hugged her tight. The safety of their arms wrapped around her filled her with warmth and comfort.

"Oh Maggie, what happened?" Mama asked with a loving look on her face.

"I... I saw... I saw something terrible today, Mama," Maggie whimpered with tears filling her eyes once more.

Her Papa looked distraught. "Come inside and tell us all about it over some warm soup."

In the kitchen, the aroma of fresh sourdough bread mingled with simmering soup was comforting. Maggie settled at the table, her fingers tracing the edges of her bowl as she shared her adventures, excitement in her voice. She spoke of meeting Drew, tasting the pink Engkala, and swinging through the trees with the orangutans. Her eyes sparkled at mention of the fruit bonanza but dimmed when she described the machines and cages.

Eager to share more, she opened her laptop and pulled up the photos. Her parents leaned in, attentive.

Her Papa's brow furrowed with concern as he studied each image, a frown tugging at his lips. Mama remained calm, her fingers resting lightly on the keyboard. She slowly absorbed the details while exchanging worried looks with the two of them.

"I have had to take down a few of these worksites in the past. These are dangerous places, Maggie. They need to be stopped immediately!" Papa said intently.

"Hang on for a moment there, dear," Mama said calmy. "We do not want to act rashly. We need to get organised."

"Look here," Maggie said as she pulled out her map. "I have pinpointed where the worksite is exactly, and how to get there from here." She pointed at the Banyan tree, the pineapple and the skull she used for the worksite.

Chapter 10

Maggie's Map

The next morning, Maggie was up at first light. She stretched her muscles and joints with her gentle morning yoga session. Fully awake and relaxed, she went straight to the kitchen. Her parents were not up yet, so Maggie got a head start and went around filling the fruit basket. She cleaned them up and made a big fruit salad with half of them and started preparing the rest to make dried fruits.

Maggie climbed up onto her chair, standing tall as she leaned over the kitchen table. She spread her crinkly map between the cereal bowls and mugs, using the milk bottle and heavy fruit bowl to keep it from curling up. With her hand on her hips, she gazed down at her map, thinking. Her eyebrows scrunched together as she tried to solve the tricky puzzle. Something was missing. It dawned on her that she needed more information about the current situation and a more detailed layout of the worksite with the comings and goings of its workers. Just then, Maggie heard the bamboo floor groan under her parents' weary footsteps.

"Good morning," her parents said simultaneously as they walked in the kitchen.

"How did you sleep last night?" Mama added.

"We were both worried you would not sleep a wink after what you have been through," Papa continued as he walked towards the coffee grinder.

Maggie sat down, looking at them with a cheerful smile. "I lay awake for a while but then realised we would find a way to help save the jungle and its inhabitants."

They were all enjoying their fruity breakfast while looking over the detailed map Maggie had laid out in the middle of the table. Maggie explained what she had figured out and asked her parents for their expertise.

"I have been thinking. If we want our efforts to work out in the long run, we are going to need your political influence, Mama." Maggie said assertively, looking across the table to her Mama's loving gaze. Lifting a spoonful of cereal and fruit to her mouth, she continued, "I remember a story you told me a couple of years ago while we were sailing across the Mediterranean Sea. It was about all your animal loving friends at the WWF and how they help safeguard animals and their ecosystems from extinction and destruction," Maggie mumbled through her mouthful of cereal. "Perhaps they would be willing to help safeguard the jungles of Borneo from further destruction?"

"I will have to go back to The Jolly Roger to use the long-range satellite radio on board," Mama replied softly as she rested her hand on Maggie's forearm, gently stroking it with her thumb.

"Papa, I think you should go back to the worksite using my map. You will notice more details than me and be able to get a better lay of the land." Maggie pointed to the map where the worksite was clearly marked with a black skull and crossbones.

He stuck his tongue out between his lips as he looked closer at Maggie's notes and sketches on the map and asked her: "What waypoints should I look out for?"

"Right here," Maggie said, pointing down at the large Banyan tree and the pineapple. "From the house, head southeast. After you walk past the mango trees and the bright pink fruit trees, continue for about an hour. You can't miss the Banyan's windy entangled tree trunk clambering to the top of the canopy. Once you've reached it, go toward the fruit field that I marked with this pineapple." Maggie put her finger down onto her map where the pineapple was drawn. "From there, you will need to head east for an hour or so before reaching the worksite."

Her parents looked at her with such pride.

"This is amazing work," her Papa said. "I'll be able to find the worksite in no time." He took out his own map and laid it over Maggie's. He started tracing the waypoints and notes onto his own map before folding it carefully.

"What will you be doing, Maggie?" he asked as he walked back through the kitchen and out onto the balcony with all his gear.

"My goal is to bring as many jungle animals together as possible. I believe our only chance of bringing peace back to these parts is with the help from the locals," Maggie said with conviction.

Chapter 11

Rango, Poppy and Eon

The dried-out bamboo pathway creaked under each of Mama's footsteps. The water in the lagoon lay low and sluggish, barely a ripple breaking the surface. Mama glanced at the stillness, knowing that the only way back to the village and The Jolly Roger was to paddle up the winding waterway ahead.

As Maggie stood there holding onto the banister, watching her Mama canoe up the windy waterway, she felt the hairs on the back of her neck stick out. As if someone, or something, was watching her. She decided to climb the nearest tree to safety, settling onto a sturdy branch. Silently and patiently, she waited for whatever was lurking in the shadows to reveal itself.

She noticed the leaves rustling in the neighbouring trees, then saw three orangutans swing out from the foliage across from the lagoon. Maggie did not recognise them. They were not from Drew's family. She remained calm and ready to hide if needed. The three orangutans stopped the second they saw her. They were hanging from the treetops over the lagoon effortlessly. The three of them were looking at each other and back at Maggie. She could only just hear what they were muttering.

"So? What do you think?" one of them muttered.

"She must be the one," the larger of the three bellowed softly as he moved in closer.

Maggie had a nagging feeling someone had been talking about her. She remained on her perch as the three orangutans swung in closer.

"Who do you think I am?" Maggie asked courageously, trying to hide her fear.

"And she can speak our tongue. She definitely is the one we have been looking for," the smallest, and probably youngest, of the three said.

"I asked you a question," Maggie said, looking them straight in the eye.

The largest of the three chuckled.

"Bosco did say you were a feisty little human. We have been wandering the jungle searching for the little human girl who was bestowed with the magical Engkala gift."

Maggie felt a little bit more at ease with her observers. They knew Bosco, this meant they knew Drew. She caught their admiring glances, but she couldn't quite grasp the reason behind it. Maggie's stomach grumbled loudly, as she looked over to the coconuts up in the next tree.

"Here you go, little girl, have this coconut," the alpha said as he grabbed a coconut and cracked it open with his bare hands. "My name is Rango. This is Poppy and Eon,"

Rango said while slowly handing the half coconut to Maggie without letting a drop of its precious water overflow. Both his gentleness and strength were remarkable.

Maggie was eager to understand why she was so important to the three of them. "Why have you been looking for me," she asked again politely, patiently awaiting their answer while drinking the coconut water and biting down onto its juicy white flesh.

"We were told you went to spy on the new worksite being set up," Rango said.

"Yes. Bosco and his troop helped me find my way there. I have seen the horrors with my own eyes," Maggie explained.

"That is exactly why we have been looking for you," the younger of the three exclaimed.

The other two looked at him in a way that meant he had spoken out of place. He instantly recoiled back behind the two others.

"Eon is right. That is one of the reasons we have been looking for you," Poppy continued.

"We need your help. The workers have caged up many of our friends and other jungle locals," Poppy said with a sad look. "We swung into Bosco and his troop, and they told us about you. A little one said you might be willing to help us."

Maggie looked at the three of them, and in that moment she felt a deep sense of validation. The jungle had truly called upon her to help save it and its inhabitants.

"I will help you free your friends and free your home," Maggie said bravely. "Follow me," she said, leading them down to her balcony. “I have started to put a plan together, and it is clear we need to gather all the help we can get from the jungle locals.”

Sceptical Collaborations

"When did Bosco and his troop tell you about me?" Maggie asked Rango. "Would you be able to track them down and convince them to join us? We are going to need every hand we can get," Maggie insisted.

Maggie had laid out her map on the balcony floor. Rango sat with his legs outstretched in front of him, his arms resting on either side of his massive furry body.

"We saw them at sunset last night. They were on their way to a protected area many weeks away," Rango muttered as he stared at the map, struggling to make sense of the tangled lines.

"Yes. Bosco mentioned he was bringing his troop south," Maggie said, confirming what Rango had just said.

"I heard about an area where the land and its inhabitants are protected from destruction and poaching!" Eon interrupted, his mouth full of the fruits dangling over the balcony.

"I read about the Sebangau National Park. It has one of the largest orangutan populations," Maggie said, worried. "That's over a thousand miles away!" She pinpointed the park's location on her map.

Poppy brought her long arms down, slamming her fists onto the bamboo floor with a thundering crash. "We should not have to move for weeks on end because of these monsters!" Poppy roared. She immediately saw the terrified look on Maggie's face. "I do apologise, little girl, all this just frustrates me so much. I do hope we find a way to keep our home from these monsters."

Poppy looked so sad. Maggie could feel the lump in her throat come back.

"We will, Poppy," she said triumphantly. "My Mama should be getting back to me on the radio soon, and my Papa should be at the worksite collecting more information. In the meantime, we need to do our best to get back in touch with Bosco and his family, as well as ask any other locals if they are willing to help us."

Maggie felt invigorated and enthusiastic. She leaned over her map, carefully pointing out small inlets leading right up to the worksite's position.

"This must be how they are navigating the dense jungle," Maggie said, analysing the map further. "My parents are out there gathering all the necessary information. Our job now is to build our team," Maggie continued authoritatively. "We are going to need three teams for this to work," she declared, her eyes bright with enthusiasm. "One team in the water, another up in the sky and a third on land, and they should all report back to me."

The three orangutans looked at her sceptically.

"We have never seen the jungle animals work together," Rango said.

"We have to try," Maggie exclaimed. "I do not know how else to get the help we need. I am sure you can find a way to save it together. After all, you all share this jungle."

They all looked at each other and agreed they should at least try.

Their conversation was interrupted by the radio going off. "Bamboo Nest, Bamboo Nest, Bamboo Nest, this is The Jolly Roger, this is The Jolly Roger, this is The Jolly Roger. Over."

Maggie jumped up and ran to the radio station. It was her Mama's voice calling from The Jolly Roger's radio station.

"Hello, Jolly Roger, this is Bamboo Nest. Over," Maggie replied in perfect radio communication.

She turned to the three orangutans, Rango, Poppy, and Eon, who looked at the radio station in amazement. They had never seen anything like this.

“My Mama is on our sailing vessel, The Jolly Roger, near the village at the end of the river. She has a radio station just like this one,” Maggie explained. “It allows us to communicate when we are far away from one another,” she went on.

They were in awe of this talking machine that allowed them to communicate over long distances.

“Listen carefully.” A tremor of fear filled Mama’s voice. “I have reached out to my contacts, and they have confirmed that the worksite seems to be an illegal one and is therefore extremely dangerous!”

Maggie’s breath quickened as she clenched her fists tightly, her expression betraying her worry.

“The men on the worksite have been hired by a mega-corporation to set up a new mining quarry,” Mama continued as calmly and clearly as she could. “Promise me you won’t go anywhere near this place alone ever again,” she said assertively.

“I promise I will not go anywhere near the worksite until we have a proper plan of action,” Maggie said reassuringly.

“You are such a smart girl,” her Mama went on. “I will be back tomorrow afternoon. Over and out.”

“Yes, no problem, I will be looking out for you. Over and out.” Maggie hung up the radio and stayed silent.

Chapter 13

Lord of the Jungle

It was time to go and pick Mama up from the waterway. Rango, Poppy and Eon had left the previous evening to find Bosco and his family.

Maggie crouched on a thick branch, her fingers gripping the rough bark, the river below shimmering as it wound through the jungle. Her gaze swept across the water until something large stirred beneath the surface, moving slow and steady. Her heart skipped, a chill creeping down her spine.

The shadow in the river faded from her mind when her Mama's canoe appeared in the distance. In an instant, Maggie swung down from her branch, her legs slicing through the air.

Mama's eyes widened, the familiar awe mixed with worry as she watched Maggie swing down from the jungle tops, landing lightly in the canoe. Maggie wrapped her arms around her, but Mama barely had time to hug her back before the canoe jolted to a stop. The sharp jerk sent them both sprawling, crashing hard onto the canoe's floor. Mama's heart raced as she scrambled to sit up, her grip tightening on Maggie, the unease settling like a knot in her chest. Something wasn't right.

"What was that?" they both whispered at the same time.

They slowly looked over the edge of the canoe on each side, when another thump rocked the canoe. Mama's heart sank when a green scaly tail broke the surface.

"Oh no," Mama shrieked. "Maggie, quickly! Climb back up into the trees." Maggie leaped up at the first hanging vines and climbed up high. She could see the outline of the giant crocodile right next to the canoe.

"Mama, you need to get up here too, there is a crocodile just next to the canoe!" Maggie shrieked as she tried dangling a large vine in her Mama's direction.

But her Mama was not able to climb like Maggie, and Maggie was not strong enough to help her. The canoe was still moving along the waterway with the current. Mama tried to steer it towards the bank. The giant reptile was following close behind without making as much as a ripple. Maggie saw the crocodile picking up speed.

"Mama, you need to hurry, it is catching up on you fast!" Maggie yelled.

Maggie heard loud rustling and branches cracking, and as quick as a flash, an orange shadow grabbed hold of Mama, carrying her up into the trees as if she were a leaf in the wind. The crocodile lunged out of the water but just missed her.

The crocodile growled, roared, and slashed the water in anger and frustration!

"How dare you save a human? Don't you realise they are destroying our home!" the crocodile bellowed.

As frightened as Maggie was, she felt ecstatic. She understood the crocodile as well as the orangutans. Maggie rushed up into the trees. She could hear the leaves and branches crack in the distance. She hurried to catch up. They were heading towards the Bamboo Nest. Maggie saw Bosco gently letting her Mama down onto the balcony. Drew was there too.

"That was too close," Bosco hooted at Mama. "You have to be more careful when navigating these waters."

Mama stared at Bosco, her face puzzled, eyes wide with disbelief. She blinked, struggling to process what had just happened. Replaying his strong hands lifting her through the air like a rag doll felt surreal. Yet, here she sat, heart pounding, gaze locked on the gentle giant who had just saved her.

"She does not understand you, Bosco," Maggie explained, as she landed on the balcony.

Bosco grunted deeply. "Be aware that the crocodile is lurking in these waters now. She has very little patience with humans. All she wants is for a safe and peaceful jungle home," he bellowed softly as he swung back up into the trees.

Chapter 14

An Eerie Introduction

Maggie moved through the treetops, searching for the canoe and her Mama's gear. She reached the area where yesterday's close call had happened. She continued swinging downriver, following the current, hoping to spot the canoe.

There it was, its bow lodged deep in the mangroves, half submerged in the muddy water. As she scanned the water below, her muscles seized as she caught sight of a ripple. Something big moved just beneath the surface, the water too still, too watchful. The crocodile might be lurking below. Reassured, Maggie knew it wouldn't matter how fast it could lunge. Up here, she was out of reach.

After she settled onto a comfortable secure spot, she waited and observed the still water surface, waiting for the tiniest ripple which would give away the crocodile's location.

The stories she had read came flooding back. The Borneo

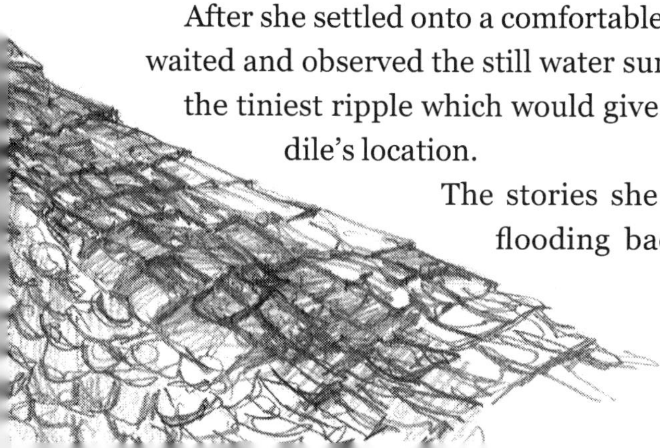

saltwater crocodile dwarfed even the largest Nile crocodile. But this was no story, this croc might be right there, waiting in the murky depths.

She racked her brain, trying to remember everything she knew about spotting crocodiles. She started looking for its nostrils popping up at the surface, or its bright yellow eyes. Those were the only way to spot a hidden crocodile on the hunt. With nothing in sight, she secured her hook to a rope, ready to collect the rucksack. The hook and rope dangled, twisting away, circling the handle, avoiding it entirely with the light breeze. She tugged on the rope but hit the canoe, making a loud thump with the heavy hook. Her heart stopped, she paused to scan the water surface, but nothing had moved.

She tugged the rope once more, this time hooking the handle. Keeping tension, she pulled it up towards her, but the bag got stuck in the tangling mangroves. She secured her rope tightly as she climbed down a little closer and tried to dislodge it. In that instance, the crocodile's entire body slowly surfaced right next to the canoe. She had been lying there, still as could be this entire time. Chills rushed down Maggie's neck. She immediately swung up to another level of branches.

As she crouched there, high up in the safety of the canopy, she thought back to what Bosco had said about the crocodile.

All she wants is for a safe and peaceful jungle home...

Maggie realised they both wanted the same thing, and a crocodile would be a great asset to her team. Maggie hesitated for a moment then climbed down to get a closer look at this dangerous, magnificent beast. She was still out of reach, but she had a clear view of the sheer size of this beautiful reptile.

"Woah, you are magnificent," she said, hoping to flatter the crocodile into starting a conversation.

She looked straight up at her and growled deeply, her bright yellow eyes fixing hers.

"I had a feeling you might come back for your belongings," she said calmly. "Enlighten me, little human. Why should I let you have them back?" The giant croc growled as she swerved her large tail onto the rucksack and the canoe.

Maggie shared every detail of her adventure with the orangutans and the dreadful worksite she had found. The crocodile lingered for a moment, her eyes watching her without much interest. She gave no sign of understanding, just drifted downriver and disappeared into the distance.

Maggie climbed down to gather her Mama's gear, left the canoe and made her way back to the house, her heart still racing from the day's events.

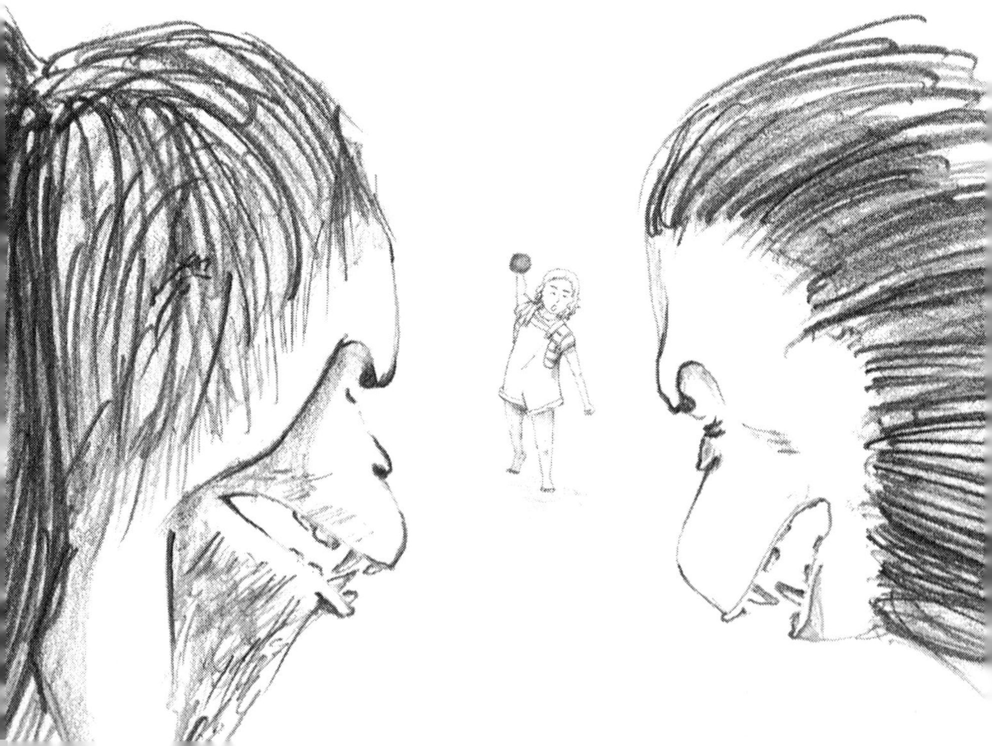

Chapter 15

Alphas Joining Forces

The next day, Maggie woke up to find her Mama on the balcony looking into the distance, holding her favourite mug. She turned to look at Maggie with a cup of hot cocoa in her hands, her feet dragging slightly as she shuffled across the kitchen still caught in a sleepy haze. They smiled at each other, enjoying the jungle waking up. The birds were cawing, the insects chirping, and other creatures were rustling around the treetops and the leafy ground. It was a magical morning with beautiful colours peering through the leaves. They felt the early warmth of each ray of sunshine on their faces. The calming jungle sounds invited peace and serenity, but they both knew of the hidden threat amidst this natural beauty.

Bosco and Rango appeared through the foliage, swinging themselves towards the Bamboo Nest. They landed onto the balcony ever so lightly. Without looking over, they shuffled around investigating. They seemed to love the fruit trees surrounding the pathway and picked a few low hanging fruits. Mama looked a little uneasy and stayed very still in her armchair, signalling Maggie to do the same.

"Don't worry, Mama, they are gentle and friendly," Maggie said reassuringly. "The big one is Rango, and the other is Bosco who saved you from the crocodile yesterday."

Mama seemed to collect herself and her face regained a little colour. She still wondered why they had come to the Bamboo Nest. They waited patiently for the two orangutans to finish eating. Bosco and Rango must have eaten half of the fruits in arm's reach before waddling over.

Bosco sat slouched with his legs out, his long heavy arms on each side of his massive body. "Rango told me about your plan to bring the jungle animals together," Bosco grunted with half a mango dripping out of his jaws, while biting down onto a whole papaya.

Maggie looked thrilled. "Yes. My idea is to build three teams. One on the water, another up above in the sky, and a third on the ground and in the trees. Together, we can put an end to the jungle's destruction!" Maggie said excitedly, forgetting her Mama could not understand the orangutan dialect.

Bosco nodded and grunted in Mama's direction. Mama smiled awkwardly at the two large apes crouching in front of her.

"I will be right back," Maggie said as she darted off to fetch her map. "Let me show you what I have figured out for now." She continued rolling it out on the bamboo floor, holding it open with the two empty mugs. Maggie went on describing her map to the two apes in English so her Mama could also understand. Rango seemed happy for a second round of explanations of the squiggly lined paper.

Mama stopped Maggie midway, “Maggie, the situation is much worse than we had anticipated. This quarry is only the newest amongst a long line of them. Over half of the jungle has been cut down, burnt, and destroyed over the past century!”

The two orangutans stared at Mama in despair, nodding in silent agreement. Sensing their sombre mood, Maggie sprang into action with determination lighting her eyes.

“We will find a way to stop any new ones from being built. The waterways are how they move about the jungle with ease. If we stop them there, we stop them everywhere!” Maggie exclaimed decisively.

“We will need to be extra careful and plan everything out properly, “Mama added. “These mega corporations will stop at nothing and some of the local authorities are under their control.”

Maggie looked over at Bosco, who seemed worried.

“I knew we should have continued south,” Bosco said. “I have risked my troop’s safety by coming back here!”

“You would have put your entire troop in even more danger by crossing so much land!” Rango interrupted.

“Do not presume that you know what is best for my troop,” Bosco roared loudly, standing up tall to face Rango.

The two alpha males were getting on the defensive and a fight was about to break out. Before anything could be done, the two alpha males were putting on a show of force. Mama grabbed Maggie by the arm and ran inside, she did not want to see where this would go. But Maggie grabbed two coconuts they had dropped and threw one at each of the huge orangutans.

"This is not the time to start fighting!" Maggie burst out. "Your home is being invaded and destroyed, and all you can do is argue amongst yourselves?"

Maggie's face twisted with anger, her brows drawing together and lips trembling as tears streamed down her cheeks. Both looked at Maggie a little puzzled. Never had anyone interrupted a fight between them. Mama wrapped her arms around Maggie to try to protect her from the two giant apes.

"Maggie is right, we need to stick together," Rango said.

"What do you suggest we do?" Bosco said, looking over to Maggie. But they were interrupted by the crackling of the radio.

Chapter 16

Eternal Fall

Mama had gone to meet up with Papa and would only be back later that day. The two alpha males had gone back to their own troops with the goal of spreading the word of creating a collaboration between all jungle locals. In the meantime, Maggie knew that having the crocodile lead the water team was crucial for asserting control over the waterways. While she was figuring this out, Drew showed up on her balcony.

She turned to her friend with a calming smile.

"You are here in the nick of time," she said with a smile. "Would you mind helping me with something essential to our cause?" she asked him hesitantly.

Drew was a little afraid of what she was going to ask him, but he agreed to listen to her request.

"You are asking a lot of me. Orangutans stay away from crocodiles. Especially large ones such as this one."

It took a little convincing and negotiating, but Drew was in, and they went to find the giant crocodile. Drew stayed up high in the treetops, while Maggie decided to walk. They found the canoe which had not moved an inch since last time. Maggie wrapped the rope around a thick branch just above the canoe and used the pully system and her friend's strength to lift it clear out of the water, draining it entirely. The two of them lingered by the water for quite some time. They wanted to turn back for lunch, but Maggie knew the crocodile would have heard all the ruckus they made when lifting the canoe up in the air.

Just then, the water surface rippled just slightly.

"Over there, did you see it?" Maggie said in a whisper.

"I did not see anything," Drew bellowed.

Maggie stared at the water, hoping to see a pair of nostrils or big yellow eyes peer over the surface. There it was, and now that she saw it, it could not be unseen. The outline of a large crocodile just beneath the surface with its two big round yellow eyes gazing at them.

Crocodiles gave Maggie the chills. What an impressive animal, such force, such stealth, the perfect predator. No wonder they have been roaming the earth since the age of the dinosaurs. She admired how gentle the crocodile seemed even though she knew how dangerous it could be when it was on the hunt.

"I have been waiting to see you again, little girl. In all my years of roaming this jungle, I have never come across a being as interesting as you," the crocodile growled with what seemed to be a grin.

"Interesting?" Maggie repeated. "What do you find so interesting about me?" she said, trying to build up a conversation. "Such a powerful being must have seen many interesting creatures roaming this jungle and its villages," Maggie said, still trying to get on the crocodile's good side.

"I see you!" the crocodile replied in an all-knowing manner. "You will not be able to win me over that easily. I have roamed these parts for over 70 years, and no one has duped me yet. Not even the mighty Nabau and all her disguises."

"Lord of the Jungle, please. Give us a moment to explain," Drew bellowed from behind Maggie.

Maggie was a little taken aback. Did Drew just call the crocodile Lord of the Jungle?

"We need your help and ancient wisdom to rid the jungle of our enemy," Drew continued. "My friend Maggie is here to help, and has a plan!"

The crocodile looked up at them with its big yellow eyes, then vanished under the surface.

Maggie was puzzled as to why Drew had called the crocodile Lord of the Jungle. She had just turned to ask him why, when the rope holding the canoe got dislodged. The canoe swung against the tree heavily, knocking Maggie off her branch. Maggie's heart sank as she fell through the air. She looked up towards Drew who threw himself towards her but just missed her hand. The fall felt like an eternity.

Her body hit the water with a huge splash. The silence and calmness of being fully submerged was terrifying, the idea of the large crocodile was even more so. Maggie closed her eyes and held her breath, frozen in fear. Just then, something huge bumped into her and brought her to the surface. Floating at the surface, she grabbed hold of a large tree trunk floating by. As she did so, the crocodile appeared next to her with all its teeth grinning at her.

Chapter 17

Home Sweet Home

Maggie's parents were walking through the jungle, on their way back to the Bamboo Nest, when they heard loud hooting calls by the waterway. Their curiosity peaked when they saw a young orangutan chaotically climbing up and down the side of a tree, frantically pointing down towards the water. Papa and Mama went closer to the water's edge and saw that their little girl had fallen in. Papa was about to jump in when Mama caught his arm and pointed to the giant crocodile right by Maggie's side. Papa did not hesitate an instant and whipped out his tranquilizer rifle. He pointed it towards the reptile and was about to shoot when Maggie saw her Papa and screamed.

"Nooooo, stoooop!" as she waved her arms in front of the crocodile's head.

The crocodile swished out of the way of his aim. Mama saw an opening and jumped in the water to save her little girl. The crocodile had disappeared into the murky depths away from Maggie and her protective parents.

Once they were both out of danger on the riverbank, Mama wrapped her arms around Maggie. Her Papa came running and wrapped his arms around them both. Drew saw his friend was safe and disappeared into the treetops.

"We'd better get home and dry you two off," Papa said shakily.

They changed into dry clothes and sat on the balcony's edge overlooking the small lagoon with a cup of hot tea. Mama paused and looked at her daughter, who seemed pensive.

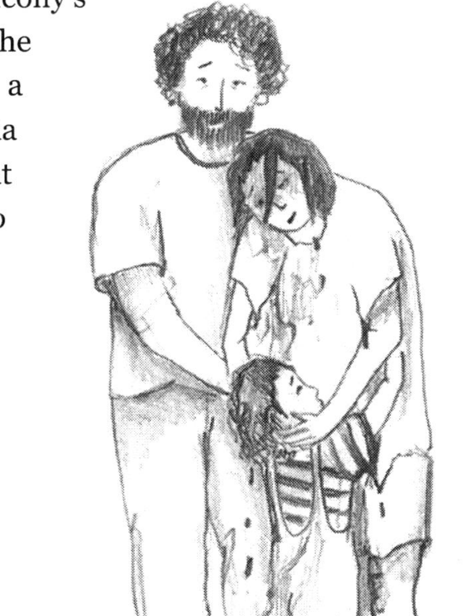

"What's on your mind, my dear?" she asked soothingly.

Maggie looked at her parents with loving eyes, then hesitated

for a second. She did not know how to explain the situation. It was an odd and spectacular one, to say the least. So, she just said what she had on her mind. She knew her parents would listen to her and would always support her and help her in any way they could.

"Ever since Drew gifted me with the magical pink Engkala fruit, I have been able to communicate and swing with the orangutans. I thought that was all I could do, but it turns out I can speak with crocodiles too," Maggie explained. "Something Bosco said the other day stuck with me. He mentioned that the crocodile's deepest desire was to regain peace and safety throughout the jungle and its waterways." Maggie paused as she lifted her gaze from her mug.

Her parents looked at her, their expressions a mix of disbelief and acceptance. Mama had witnessed firsthand Maggie communicating with the two large alpha male orangutans.

Maggie went on to explain what she had understood about the waterways and their importance to the quarry development. Maggie's Papa put a gentle hand on her shoulder.

"I saw the waterways too. I also noticed how important they are to the quarry men. Without them, they cannot move in or out of the worksite," Papa agreed, in his usual soothing tone.

"Exactly!" Maggie cried out. "This is why I went out searching for the crocodile with Drew. I was taking every precaution I could think of, and everything was going great until..." Maggie stopped to think. "I had secured the canoe vertically from a large sturdy branch, but my knot got dislodged. I fell through the air into the water. I could see the canoe hurtling towards me, and the crocodile whipped its tail, making the canoe bounce off away from me." Maggie looked up at her parents, eyes wide with excitement. "The crocodile saved me!" she blurted out.

Maggie saw Papa wipe a tear from his eye. She had never seen him cry before. She hugged him tightly and Mama joined in the family hug. Maggie realised they must have been terrified to find her in the water with a crocodile.

"I'm sorry for having frightened you," Maggie wept.

"Don't worry about it, my dear," Mama replied. "You are safe now, and that is what matters," her Mama whispered softly.

"But you need to promise us not to put yourself in danger like that again," Papa interjected lovingly. "Crocodiles are not known for their docility," he went on, making it clear he wanted Maggie to take extra precautions when it came to the crocodile.

"I promise," Maggie said gently. "But I believe the crocodile will be our greatest ally to control the waterways."

Chapter 18

Team Expansion

Their family hug was interrupted by a deep grunting sound rising from below. The sound rippled through the air, snapping them out of their moment. They exchanged glances and moved towards the balcony banister, searching the dense foliage beneath. Shadows flickered between the trees, but nothing moved. Curiosity took hold of them as they walked quietly around the Bamboo Nest's pathway, only to hear the grunting echoed from deeper in the underbrush.

"It seems like it is coming from the ground," Maggie said as she carefully leaned over the rail.

"Little girl," a deep growling voice said. "It is I, Dhia. The crocodile, Lord of the Jungle."

"It's the crocodile," Maggie said excitedly to her parents.

The three of them hurried to the lift. Papa took control of the lowering mechanism, determined to keep Mama and Maggie out of danger. As the lift slowly descended, he brought it to a slow steady stop about 20 feet from the ground. They peered through the lift's bamboo bars, eyes widening at the site of the massive reptile. It looked so much bigger on land. They could hear each thumping step it took as it carried its heavy body over the leafy ground.

Suddenly, a rustling in the trees ahead caught their attention. Drew swung down to see Maggie.

"Maggie, I have good news!" he bellowed energetically.

"Drew! Be careful! The crocodile is just there," Maggie said, pointing down towards the reptile.

"I know! That is my good news. I went to find her after you were safely back on land with your parents," Drew grunted, before climbing back up to the pathway and indulging in the balcony fruits.

Maggie turned to her parents and explained what Drew had just said. They remained sceptical about their daughter getting involved with such a powerful crocodile, a creature historically renowned for being relentlessly dangerous. They were still getting used to their daughter, the animal whisperer. They decided to give their daughter a chance, so Papa brought the lift a little closer to the ground, remaining out of the crocodile's reach.

"Aah, there you are!" Dhia bellowed as she turned to Maggie. "Let me introduce myself properly. I am Dhia, and I have roamed these parts since I was born in a lagoon just like this one. I have watched so many friends come and go. And sadly, I have seen our jungle home get torn apart year after year by humans and their destructive ways." She growled softly. "Both my parents were captured and taken away on a huge barge with its loud, smoky engines. That day changed everything for me. Since then, I have hidden away, trying to keep my distance from humans," Dhia continued, her eyes growing distant and sad. "But it is getting harder to stay out of their way. They are taking more and more of our jungle home. We can barely move from one spot to another without crossing paths with their deadly machines."

Maggie was looking at the crocodile in despair. She could not even start to understand what this poor creature had had to endure throughout her lifetime.

"I think we can help each other." Maggie held her breath, awaiting the Lord of the Jungle's response as she swung out of the caged lift onto an overhanging branch.

The crocodile paused for a moment, then slid back into the lagoon as she narrowed her gaze upon Maggie. Maggie kept her eyes fixed on her observer, ready to swing out of the way.

"Help each other out?" Dhia growled loudly after a minute or so. She was already aware of Maggie's idea for uniting the jungle locals but wanted to hear it from her. “What do you have in mind?” Dhia asked Maggie, keeping an overzealous tone.

Maggie knew at once she had gained Dhia’s full attention.

Chapter 19

Masterplan Part 1

The next morning was buzzing with excitement. Maggie walked into the kitchen with a skip in her step, her heart racing with energy. Her parents were sitting at the table waiting for her. The sun streamed through the windows, and the whole house seemed ready for action.

"If we are going to strategise our plan correctly, we should head to the patio by the lagoon," Maggie said with a grin. "We will need everyone's ideas, and I believe Dhia is already waiting for us down there."

Mama and Papa exchanged worried looks.

"I will agree to the patio," Mama said slowly. "But we will keep the gate closed. Dhia may be friendly, but she is still a wild crocodile." Papa nodded in agreement.

They gathered everything they needed, maps, notebooks and photos, as they moved to the small patio overlooking the lagoon. The air was thick with the smells of the jungle. Birds squawked overhead, and the water shimmered beneath the hot sun. Dhia's massive body floated just beneath the surface.

Papa spread out a large map where he pinned photos detailing every aspect of the worksite. He pointed out where the animals were caged, the access points to the waterway, and the best infiltration routes. Maggie leaned forward, eyes wide with focus. Her pulse quickened as she saw the danger laid out before them.

"My plan is simple," she started. "Three teams working together. One to control the waterways and rivers, another to infiltrate the worksite to free the animals and scare the workers away, and the third in the sky ensuring smooth communication between all teams."

Papa, Mama and Dhia nodded as Maggie outlined the details.

"The first step is to stop the workers by blocking the waterways. While they are stuck, we will free the animals, whether they are trapped at the worksite, or already being shipped to larger vessels on the river." Maggie's voice was filled with determination now, but her eyes betrayed her worried mind. "We must move fast. When I was at the worksite, I saw a couple of Storm's storks being brutally caged up. If we could find their flock, maybe they would be willing to help us save their friends," Maggie added hopeful.

Dhia's eyes gleamed from the water. "I know where to possibly find their flock," she said in her deep, rumbling voice. "But they like to stay hidden, especially from crocodiles. Once I have located their nesting grounds, I will need you to come with me to talk to them and convince their queen to help the cause."

Papa frowned protectively. "I'm not sure it is safe for Maggie to go alone."

"I will guard her with my life," Dhia said firmly. "After all, we won't be able to save our jungle without Maggie leading the teams."

Mama and Papa shared a glance, then looked at Maggie. Their faces softened. After those words, they had no choice but to trust their daughter, and who better to protect her than a giant saltwater crocodile.

"Okay," Papa finally said. "But be careful."

Mama nodded as she rummaged through a tiny black box. "If the storks agree to help, I suggest you convince them to wear these tiny radio transmitters." She picked up the devices and handed one to Maggie, "You would be able to communicate with them from a distance."

Papa smiled, already examining the devices. "I can modify these easily so we can all have one. How many do we have?"

"Just a few," Mama replied.

"Perfect. I will have them ready by morning."

Suddenly, a low growl filled the air. Everyone froze and Dhia sank below the surface. Maggie looked up, her senses tingling. A shadow moved through the trees, silent and sleek. A leopard was stalking them, inching closer, hidden in the jungle canopy. Her parents hadn't noticed yet, but Maggie could feel it watching them.

Before she could warn them, the giant cat leapt from the shadows, landing on the patio. Mama screamed as Papa shot to his feet, fear flashing across his face. Dhia resurfaced, her sharp eyes locked on the leopard. The big cat quickly backed up, keeping a safe distance from the crocodile.

"I heard someone here is trying to save our jungle," the leopard purred, his voice smooth as silk.

Maggie stood tall, her fear slipping away.

"You have heard correctly," she said, her voice steady. "And you have come at just the right time."

The leopard's golden eyes narrowed.

"What do you mean?"

"We need someone smart and sneaky to spy on a new worksite being set up. Someone who can move unseen."

The leopard circled them slowly, then stopped.

"I can do that," he hissed before leaping back into the trees, vanishing as quickly as he had appeared.

"Wait! How will we find you again?" Maggie called after him.

"I need to get ready. I will come back tomorrow morning," his voice echoed from the shadows.

The jungle fell silent again, the tension easing. Mama shook her head, still in shock.

"What just happened?"

"We found our ground spy," Maggie said, smiling. "And he's very good at disappearing."

Papa laughed, wrapping Maggie in a big hug. "You are brilliant!"

They quickly turned back to the map. Maggie's brow furrowed. "We still need muscle to deal with the machines, and to chase the workers away."

Dhia raised her head proudly. "I know a herd of jungle elephants. Their matriarch will help us. I am certain of it."

Maggie's heart soared. Everything was coming together. They spent the rest of the day refining their plan, as the sun slowly dipped low over the horizon.

Chapter 20

Masterplan Part 2

Maggie woke early the next morning, her excitement bubbling over. Today was the day they would begin. The Bamboo Nest was quiet, her parents still asleep. Maggie spent a few moments writing in her notebook, organizing her thoughts.

By mid-morning, everyone gathered at the patio by the lagoon. Azrul, the clouded leopard had returned, silent as ever. He slunk in from the shadows, his golden eyes gleaming.

Maggie took a deep breath.

"Alright, let's get to work. Dhia, you will oversee the waterfront. Build your team and organise blockades to limit all the workers' movements," Maggie said, pointing to the best blockade locations on her map. "You will also need to speak to the elephants and bring them in on the plan. And once you have located the storks, together we will go find their queen and convince her to lead the sky team," Maggie said assertively.

"Consider it done." Dhia nodded as she immediately got to her tasks, using her low frequency vibrations to communicate across the waterways to all the other reptiles.

Maggie turned to her parents.

"Mama, you and Papa should go back to the village. This time, get in contact with the village chieftains to let them know what is happening. Try not to get the political authorities' attention. They might be the ones involved with the mega-corporation. Report back any anomalies or information you deem important."

"Of course," Papa said with a smile. "We will make sure to warn the chieftains, so they do not get in the way, and keep the villagers safe."

Finally, Maggie looked at Azrul.

"You will spy on the worksite. We need to know everything, how many workers there are, what they are doing, and how many animals are still caged at the worksite, and if any have been moved to boats on the wider river."

Azrul flicked his tail. "I have already gathered a few friends to help me. We will cover every corner of the worksite and report back."

"That's perfect." Maggie's heart raced with excitement.

Before they headed out, Maggie opened the small black box. Inside were the tiny radios Papa had modified.

She held one up, showing Dhia and Azrul how she wore hers around her right ear.

"With these around your necks or behind your ear, we will be able to stay in contact. If anything does not go to plan, let me know immediately."

Dhia did not hesitate, nodding her giant head. Azrul eyed the device suspiciously but eventually crouched down, allowing Maggie to place the collar around his neck. His muscles tensed as it clicked into place.

"It is a bit uncomfortable," he muttered, his long fangs showing as he spoke.

Maggie smiled softly. "It will help us stay safe. Just give it a try."

With the radios in place, the teams set off. Maggie watched them go, her heart filled with hope. But she knew deep down they would need more help if they were to succeed.

Just then, a soft buzzing filled the air. Maggie's ears pricked up. She recognised the sound instantly, the quick fluttering of a blue-eared kingfisher. She followed the sound, spotting the tiny bird darting around the patio.

"Hi there," Maggie whispered, watching it zip back and forth. The kingfisher hovered in front of her, its bright feathers flashing in the sunlight. Then, in a blur of motion, it shot into the jungle.

Maggie smiled to herself. "Maybe you can help us too."

She sat back, already thinking of how the kingfisher could fit into their plan. The jungle was coming to life around her, and their fight to save it had only just begun.

NOC-NOC

Chapter 21

Noc–Noc

A few miles upriver, Dhia and her team were gathering intel on the comings and goings of the boats and barges.

Dhia had seen a lot of these barges appearing for the first time in the 1970s. Back then, the jungle and rivers were pristine and only a few villages cohabited within the jungle water maze.

A loud clunk echoed through the air, followed by a heavy thudding that reverberated across the water. Dhia's muscles coiled as her tail slashed powerfully through the water, sending waves crashing on all sides. Her jagged jaws snapped open as she spun, her eyes piercing the murky depths with a cold, primal intensity.

Dhia's golden eyes caught movement across the still waters. Her massive body sank just below the surface until only her eyes and nostrils remained visible. Her powerful tail moved in slow, fluid strokes as she propelled herself forward. The water barely rippled in her wake. The sharp tang of oil pricked her senses, a scent she knew but could not place.

Noc-Noc, the humans' dredging barge, emerged from behind the bend. Memories came crashing over Dhia like a wave. The deafening roar of the machines, the destruction it had brought to her home, tearing through the mangroves, widening rivers for human construction. This monstruous intruder had desecrated her world.

Dhia's chest tightened with a mix of anger and anxiety as she stared at the vessel. She pushed her painful memories aside, forcing herself to focus on the task ahead. She signalled a pair of small green snakes lurking nearby to approach it unnoticed and get eyes on the Noc-Noc. The snakes slipped silently into the water, vanishing beneath the surface.

As she waited, Dhia realised she might need more help to tackle this threat. For now, she braced herself, her fury simmering beneath her resolve as she awaited the snakes' report.

Chapter 22

Kingfishers

Meanwhile, in the vibrant heart of the jungle, Maggie swung through the trees. Her fingers deftly gripping the sturdy vines along the waterway near the Bamboo Nest. Sunlight filtered through the dense canopy, casting dappled shadows across the jungle. A faint buzzing filled the air, and high-pitched, voices chirped

around the jungle canopy. Maggie sensed the chirping and buzzing was about her.

"Over there! Up in the trees." A tiny dark blue shadow chirped as it whizzed by rapidly.

"That is no human." Another blue shadow chirped.

"Look at it moving through the jungle tops. It must be an ape of some kind," the buzzing continued.

The buzzing got louder and closer. Maggie recognised it and looked around to spot her blue-eared kingfisher overlookers.

"I can hear you, but I cannot see you," Maggie said inquisitively. "Would you mind coming over to me?" she asked, hopeful to meet them up close.

She hung from a large vine, looking around as a realm of kingfishers appeared around her.

"I told you she could communicate with us," one of them called out.

They all settled down and found a comfortable perch in front of Maggie. A lengthy conversation started where Maggie recounted her Bornean story and what her unconventional team of jungle animals were trying to accomplish.

"I like this one. You were right to bring us together to meet her," the most colourful kingfisher chirped. He buzzed right up to Maggie. "We will join your unconventional team of jungle heroes."

Maggie smiled. "I suggest you join Azrul the clouded leopard and his spies. You would be a major help to him. I would need one of you to be willing to wear this tiny radio transmitter," she said, holding the tiniest of the radios between her fingers.

With that said, they buzzed off as quickly as they appeared, with the most colourful kingfisher proudly wearing the transmitter.

Chapter 23

The Meeting

Maggie felt it was essential to hold a secondary meeting and quickly spread the word. The late afternoon sun cast long shadows on the bamboo deck. The skies were a brilliant blue, but the air was heavy with humidity. The team arrived one by one.

"Have any of you heard from my parents?" Maggie asked, slightly distressed.

The team fell silent, the lack of information was puzzling and distressing.

"I'm sure they are OK," Dhia growled, trying to sound reassuring. "Why don't you try to contact them with your radio station?" Dhia suggested.

Maggie jumped over the gate, onto the pathway and ran up to the kitchen to use the Bamboo Nest's radio station.

Maggie came back down the pathway, her feet dragging and her face a mask of disbelief. She looked at her team, struggling to find the words as tears welled in her eyes. The silence enveloped her, and she felt lost, unable to articulate the chaos swirling in her mind. Just then, her emotions overwhelmed her, and she broke into tears.

"They left a distress signal saying they were kidnapped and taken to a boat on the river!" Maggie exclaimed, her voice trembling with urgency. The alarming news hung in the air, creating a palpable tension as her team absorbed the shocking revelation.

Drew wrapped his warm, long, hairy arms around comfortingly.

"Do not worry, Maggie. I have just sent a couple of kingfishers to find out where they are. We will rescue them with all the others!" Azrul said assuredly.

"You are right. My parents are not the only ones who are in danger. We need to keep our eyes on target," Maggie said, more determined than ever.

Everyone was spellbound by Maggie's assertiveness. The team was invigorated and ready to get going.

The meeting stretched on, the moon climbing steadily across the night sky, casting a silvery glow on their faces. Tension hung in the air as each member took turns sharing updates about their teams. Dhia floated forwards as she spoke about the dredging vessel Noc-Noc. The light caught the determination in her eyes, and the others listened intently, their faces illuminated by the moonlight.

Azrul, sitting back with an air of calm intensity, nodded as he shared his own progress.

"I have silently surrounded the worksite," he said, his voice low but firm. "Ready to infiltrate it and rescue the prisoners."

A low tremor rippled through the ground sending shivers across the lagoon's water surface. The team tensed, eyes scanning the surroundings for the source of the disturbance. Suddenly, a dark shadow emerged on the opposite bank, moving with an ominous grace. As it approached, the silhouette gradually stepped into the moonlight, revealing more of its form with each deliberate stride. The silhouette transformed into a massive jungle elephant, its colossal frame now visible as it approached the Bamboo Nest, its curious gaze locking onto the unconventional team.

Dhia's call for help had reached the elephant matriarch, who made her way to the Bamboo Nest to meet the jungle's young saviour. Her arrival was a momentous occasion, as the team welcomed her with a mixture of awe and gratitude, sharing the vital information that had just been discussed. With a powerful presence, the matriarch joined Azrul's land team, tasked with overpowering the heavy machinery and creating chaos among the workers.

As the meeting ended, the gravity of their mission settled in. One by one, they returned to their nests, a sense of purpose igniting their way. Maggie walked back to her house and curled up in her parents' bed, enveloped in the familiar warmth of their blanket. In that cocoon of comfort, she felt a glimmer of hope, knowing the jungle had a formidable team as an ally.

Chapter 24

A Legend's Story

Maggie was about to fall asleep when the hairs on the back of her neck stood up, and a shiver went all the way down her spine to her toes. She lifted her head ever so slightly from her pillow and saw two huge yellow splinter eyes staring at her from the bedroom window. She jumped to her feet ready to get to safety. She could clearly see an oval shadowy face seamlessly floating in the darkness of the night. Maggie thought she was dreaming or in a nightmare of some sort. She thought she could hear a slight slithering and hissing sound.

She stood there, frozen in place, and in the blink of an eye the shadowy figure disappeared into the darkness. She turned on the night light and went to the kitchen for a glass of water. The balcony candle was still shining brightly and repelling all the biting insects. The chilly night air sent another shiver down her body as she went out onto the balcony.

"My dear girl," said a resonant jungle voice. "I mean you no harm," the slither continued.

There was a calm assurance about the sound of this voice. It pulled Maggie towards it as if it were a compass pulling the needle north. Maggie snapped out of her trance.

"Who is out here?!" Maggie said in an assertive tone.

Out from the darkness, the largest head Maggie had ever seen was rising from the jungle floor 30 feet below. Maggie wanted to run but her legs would not move. She wanted to scream but her voice was silent. She was petrified!

"I told you not to be frightened, little girl. If I were going to have you as a snack, I would have done it by now," the beast hissed in a laughing manner. "I am here to measure you up to see if you are ready for the task ahead."

The creature came into the moonlight and Maggie could see her observer's entire body. Maggie remembered Zikri's tale of legend and what her good friend Dhia had told her. She mustered all the courage she could.

"Are you the Legendary Nabau? The python goddess of Borneo?" she asked.

The snake lifted one side of her huge mouth, making it seem like a half smile of some kind.

"You must be! How many majestic pythons are roaming this jungle?" Maggie said, nervously bringing humour and flattery to the situation.

"You are correct, my dear girl. I once was the guardian of these parts," she said in a defeated tone.

Maggie confidently moved closer to the spectacular being, carefully watching her eyes which were following each of her movements.

"So," Maggie began, "if what Dhia has told me and what I have read is true, you must be the new protector of the land, water, people, and animals of Borneo?" Maggie said inquisitively.

Maggie kept a fixed and stern gaze on those big yellow eyes. Nabau looked back into Maggie's gaze.

"I have been known to keep the peace in the region." She seemed beaten down when she hissed those words.

"What's wrong?" Maggie asked empathically.

Nabau had a pensive look about her. She was gazing into her past and was remembering every little detail.

"If you are not overly tired, I can tell you a story," Nabau said in a mysterious voice as she coiled up onto a few overreaching trunk-size branches.

Maggie sat down in her armchair, the warmth and softness of her blanket bringing comfort to the evening chill, and Nabau started.

"Life is a precious gift no matter how much time we each have on this beautiful planet we all call home. We need to respect our home as best we know how, as it is the oldest living being that surrounds us and gives us all life and meaning."

Nabau's voice was mesmerising and in some way hypnotic. Maggie was holding on to each word her new friend was saying. "I remember as far back as my first few months in this forest. I have never felt so alone in my entire 1,000 years of roaming our planet than over the last century. I never knew my mother, nor my father, and I am not sure exactly how I came to be." Nabau was pensive again.

"A thousand years old?" Maggie interrupted abruptly.

"Yes, my dear girl, and I don't know what my age span should be seeing as I am the only one of my kind as far as I know," she said sadly. Maggie was in awe to be in the presence of a legend. "Living for such a long time is a gift but also a curse, my dear girl. You see, with all the beauty our home has to offer, its inhabitants have created so much pain and misery amongst themselves.

"Sadly, I must admit I have become a little dulled out by it all, which might explain why I have left my birthplace to be destroyed by deforestation and disrespectful occupation. I used to share this island with an ancient tribe of humans, amidst the numerous other jungle animals. We used to roam freely anywhere we pleased. Unfortunately, we had to start remaining inland, and far from the coastline where pirates would invade, pillage and kidnap many of the island locals.

"Then, a few hundred years ago, outside settlers came to the island. This was the beginning of the end for our beautiful, peaceful jungle home. I left Borneo when a war so destructive began and atrocities were being committed daily. I helped save many of my friends and local villagers, but rumours of my existence quickly spread, and a reward was promised to whomever brought my head back to the invaders. It quickly became unsafe for me to stay here. I only wish I could have taken others with me. I knew deep down that my journey was a perilous and dangerous one."

Nabau was deep into her memories. She noticed Maggie was falling asleep. She stopped her storytelling and wrapped her in her coil to keep her warm.

A branch cracked and some leaves rustled, Nabau was alert again but did not move from her perch. She remained there silently looking into the darkness, knowing what was there. Maggie awoke from her slumber, wondering why Nabau had stopped her storytelling. She heard the rustling of leaves in the distance. Something was heading their way fast.

"Don't worry, little girl, your young friend is on his way here. I will see you soon." With those last words, Nabau was gone as silently as she had arrived.

Chapter 25

Splash of Hope

Maggie stood up as Drew appeared from the darkness and stepped onto the balcony. He seemed beaten down and worried.

"What's wrong?" she asked him consolingly.

He was panting loudly.

"We were silently lying low on the outskirts of the work-site when our troop was ambushed by a group of poachers." Drew was shuffling around the balcony erratically.

Maggie walked up to him and lay her hand on his shoulder. She took his hand into hers and looked deeply into his eyes. She wrapped her arms around his body, trying to calm him down.

"Try to breathe. Follow my own breathing." Maggie emphasised her breathing in with her arm and breathing back out again. "There you go, relax your breathing. Your thoughts will relax too."

Maggie had enchanted her friend with her calming wisdom. His panting stopped as he sat down on the deck.

"We were silently watching from the trees, and in a flash, chaos broke out. Weighted nets were being thrown, friends and family were being pulled out of the canopy, crashing to the ground. It happened so fast I barely managed to escape. I was surrounded by three of the workers when my mother charged them, shrieking to swing away and to get you!" Drew let out a yelping roar as he said those words.

Drew was still in shock. Maggie could see it and feel it in his trembling voice.

"Oh no, that's horrible, Drew! I am so sorry to hear this happened."

Maggie was so riled by the news, her tiredness had left her body, but she could see Drew needed to rest and eat. She set him up inside the safety of her home and gave him some freshly picked fruits and some water. Maggie noticed dawn was breaking, so no time could be wasted.

"Stay here, my friend, you need to rest. I need to meet up with Dhia. Too many of our families are being imprisoned. We need to get the storks on board and infiltrate the worksite soon!" Maggie said forcefully and compassionately.

Maggie met up with Dhia by the main river not too far from the village. As she was explaining what had happened to Drew's family, Maggie noticed a lot of commotion and large boats lined up blocking the entire river from bank to bank.

"What is happening over there?" Maggie asked, perplexed by the number of boats.

"I am not sure how it happened, but the large dredging vessel sunk and is blocking the entire river for vessels to reach the sea," Dhia said. "I went to have a closer look and the wreckage is impressive. The entire body of the vessel is contorted like a crushed soda can," Dhia added.

"It seems as if it was sunk and placed perfectly to block any vessel from coming in from the open ocean or heading out," Maggie commented, intrigued.

"I only know of one creature powerful enough to sink so large a vessel and create such a wreckage," Dhia said solemnly. "But I have not seen or heard from Nabau in decades," she went on.

"I think you might be right, my friend," Maggie grinned, showing all her teeth. "Your friend Nabau came to visit me last night."

Dhia's face lit up! She roared, splashed, lashed, and swirled around in the water. Maggie had never seen Dhia this happy and excited.

"If Nabau is back, the workers do not stand a chance," Dhia continued, exhilarated. "By crushing the Noc-Noc dredger and blocking the river in and out, the humans won't be able to create new waterways or access any of their quarries scattered around the jungle."

"We need to get a move on in, finding the queen stork," Maggie reminded Dhia. "Have you found their nesting grounds yet?" she asked, hopeful.

Dhia flashed a grin as she smoothly eased Maggie up onto her broad scaly back. Maggie caught her breath, a mix of thrill and wonder settling over her as she found her balance. She trailed her fingers across Dhia's rugged scales, tough and worn like old leather. Beneath her touch, scars crisscrossed Dhia's back, stories from battles long past etched into her skin. With a smooth powerful push, Dhia glided forward, slicing through the river's surface like a shadow. Maggie's eyes widened, the familiar banks falling away as they ventured upriver into unknown territory. The thrill of discovery sparked in Maggie's chest.

Chapter 26

Her Majesty

Dhia had swum out from the main river into a tiny inlet. She could barely fit her large body through the narrowest parts and had to crawl over the shallowest bits while Maggie crouched down low onto Dhia's back to fit under the thick jungle bushes.

"Are we there yet?" Maggie said, struggling to stay on top of Dhia's back while fighting off the vines, branches and other overgrown plants hanging over the waterway.

"We have just entered the storks' territory," Dhia said in a whisper.

They were out in the open now and Maggie could see the flock of Storm's storks in the distance. She found her balance and stood up straight. She spread her feet as wide apart as she could over Dhia's back, trying to use the large scales to fix her feet on. Maggie held her head as high as she could, hoping to be seen and maybe even be recognised by one of the storks. As Dhia had feared, the second the flock noticed her, they flew up high into the sky.

Maggie sat back down with her feet dangling over into the water on either side of the giant crocodile's body.

"What will we do now?" Maggie said in despair.

They both seemed to be in dismay and at a loss with the outcome and the possibilities ahead. Without the eyes in the sky, it will make it that much more difficult to outmanoeuvre the workers.

"Come in, Maggie. This is Azrul." Maggie's radio went off with some loud static.

"I can hear you. I am with Dhia," she replied.

"The kingfishers have found your parents. The latest sighting was on one of the barges heading to the ocean."

Maggie was distraught but relieved to know where her parents were.

"Thank you, Azrul. Did you see any other prisoners with my parents?" Maggie asked, concerned about Drew's family.

"No, we were not able to get a closer look."

"OK. Dhia and I will get a rescue mission on the way. In the meantime, get your team ready then meet back up with us at the Nest. Dhia and I still need to get the storks to join our efforts."

Maggie and Dhia found themselves drifting by the entrance to the waterway which led to Maggie's house. Dhia started paddling ever so lightly to slip into the waterway's drift when a large stork flew overhead and started circling. It flew lower and lower until it was right above them, using its wingspan to hover right there with the breeze, casting its large shadow over them.

They continued along the waterway to Maggie's home in silence, knowing they were being closely followed.

"I am willing to discuss the cause with you now," a pretentious voice shrieked.

Dhia remained cool headed as she continued gliding forward through the murky water. Maggie, on the other hand was scanning the riverbanks and the treetops to find the queen stork. They arrived in the lagoon and Maggie got off onto the patio. Dhia remained in the water floating just below the surface. The queen stork landed on an overreaching branch and walked closer to them.

"I am grateful you are taking a leap of faith and trusting us," Maggie said, breaking the awkward silence. "Let's go up onto the balcony. Dhia, I'll open the gates for you to walk up the pathway." Maggie suggested, creating a welcoming atmosphere for the queen.

The three of them went up to the balcony, where they found Drew still resting. He woke up in shock to find the three of them looking at him.

"I must have dozed off for a moment." He yawned and turned to Maggie for reassurance. "Have you heard anything about my family?" he asked with a trembling voice.

"Not yet, Drew. While we wait for Dhia's team and the kingfishers to report back, our newest member might be able to give us some insight into the situation," Maggie replied, and looked up to the queen stork.

She was perched on a high branch, not wanting to be too close to Dhia, or the rest of them for that matter.

"I would rather discuss another incident for the time being!" she said as she turned her gaze to Maggie.

Both were taken aback by the lack of empathy in her majesty's reply.

"You are here asking for my help when you were clearly seen watching two of my friends get brutally imprisoned by fellow humans at that dreadful place!" she said, glaring at her from her high perch. "Do you deny it?"

Dhia was about to snap, when luckily Maggie noticed and jumped in elegantly.

"Your highness, if I may. I remember perfectly the day I saw the worksite for the first time and heard the dreadful shrieks of distress the two storks were making while being so violently caged up. I wish I could have done something to help them then and there, but I would have just been thrown into a cage myself. Your two friends are part of the reason I am standing here today, working hard to free not only your friends but your entire jungle from these monsters. These workers may be fellow humans, but I do not call them my friends!" Maggie felt invigorated. Her blood was pumping and her determination bubbling up.

She did not want to show it, but the queen liked Maggie. She elegantly glided down to the balcony deck.

"Coming back to the other night's ambush. I saw the whole thing happen and your family were being recklessly unsafe," she continued, lifting her beak up imperiously to Drew.

"Now you listen here, stork!" Drew burst out. "I don't know who you think you are, but my family did not deserve to get attacked by the jungle invaders. Just like your friends did not deserve it either!" Drew bellowed out until the stork interrupted.

"Jungle invaders, you say!" Her voice carried loudly around the balcony and stopped Drew on the spot. "And you would know so much about these jungle invaders from your many years of roaming the jungle treetops," the queen said with a chuckle and a grin.

"I would know more than any of you combined," a deep, entrancing voice muttered from the jungle depths.

Maggie recognised the voice immediately. The stork went still, feathers pressed tight to her sides. Everyone else, Dhia included, seemed to shrink instinctively. Their bodies tense and low as though they were hoping to melt into the bamboo floor. Silence thickened around them, each creature frozen, breaths shallow, as if caught in the gaze of a predator.

"You dare question another Bornean local when you come and go as you deem fit, Nuurul!"

At the sound of her name, her majesty's eyes went wide with terror, every feather stiffening. Yet, she dared not flee. Nabau's immense, scaly body coiled around the house, encircling it from the ground up. A living barrier casting shadows across the bamboo balcony.

"I...I...was..." Nuurul stuttered incomprehensibly.

"You were being obnoxious and unqueenly, my dear," Nabau slithered bluntly.

"I was. Please forgive me, oh great Nabau," she said with a trembling voice.

"I do not believe I am the one you should be apologising to," Nabau retorted.

Maggie noticed a slight twitch in the stork's eye when being told to apologise to Drew. With a tightness in her posture, the queen turned, feathers ruffling slightly as she gracefully folded herself down. Her long, elegant neck lowered toward Drew. Her beak dipped as she knelt, her voice a soft murmur as she offered her apology.

Chapter 27

The Ambush Part 1

They all stared in awe at Nabau's colossal form looming before them.

"My dear friends, we must set aside our quarrels," Nabau murmured, her voice deep and powerful. "Our home depends on it."

Maggie stepped forward, holding the last radio transmitter. "Nuurul, I need you to wear this around your neck," she explained as she pointed to the one she had behind the ear. "It will allow us to communicate at all times."

Reluctantly, Nuurul agreed as she allowed Maggie to strap it at the base of her long neck. Maggie looked around at her team leaders.

"Alright. Is everyone clear on what they must do?" Maggie asked, scanning their faces.

One by one they nodded, determined and ready.

"The time has come to save your jungle," Maggie declared, standing tall.

With a mighty beat of her wings, Nuurul soared into

the sky, rejoining her flock who awaited her command.

Dhia swam out of the lagoon toward the river, on her way to let her team know it was time to set the blockades.

Azrul vanished into the jungle shadows, racing to join his team in preparation to infiltrate the worksite.

Maggie, Drew and Nabau were the last ones left. Drew's expression was tense, the thought of going back to the worksite lingering in the back of his mind.

"Just stay by my side, Drew," Maggie reassured him. "We are in this together."

"We should get moving," Maggie said. "Drew and I will head to the worksite first. Nabau, I suggest you go to the river in case Dhia needs help with the larger vessels."

Maggie and Drew were almost upon the worksite's edge when they slowed their swinging.

Drew looked to Maggie. "Where is everybody?" he asked, puzzled.

Maggie glanced at Drew, signalling him to stop moving forwards and to be as quiet as he could.

Just then, Azrul pounced up to their level in the trees and grinned. "I brought some climbing friends who are eager to help," he purred, leaning his paw in the trees to where a group of lemurs and proboscis monkeys were hanging. "The elephants are a bit further back to avoid giving our position away," Azrul said firmly.

"Dhia? Can you hear me?" Maggie whispered into her earpiece.

"Loud and clear, my friend. My team is in place ready to go," Dhia growled, eager to get started.

"OK, everyone, go do your thing!" Maggie commanded.

***

Dhia was right by the main port, where all the quarry loads were taken before heading out to the open seas. Her team was ready to ambush any smaller barges before they could reach the larger shipping vessels.

The water team had set up blockades running all the way from the tiniest inland waterways to the open ocean. Just after Dhia had scrambled her team, something caught her attention on the other opposite riverbank. Small boats were bringing caged animals out from the waterway in a hurry. With a decisive flick of her tail, she led a couple of monitor lizards to intercept them, stopping them midway across the river.

The villagers gathered along the riverbank, drawn in by all the commotion.

“Remember, no one is to be harmed,” Maggie’s voice echoed through the radio transmitters. “We are here to show the world you are a force to be reckoned with, but you are not a threat to them.”

Dhia ordered her team to force the workers off their boats but not harm them, and even help the ones who could not swim. This took immense self-control on behalf of her team but it showed respect and care to the local workers. The idea was to engage on a respectful level with the men and women who were only following orders. In a way, they were also captives from the quarry businesses.

The scene was out of a story book, the onlookers could not believe their eyes when they saw a group of lizards, snakes and crocodiles safely bringing quarry workers back to shore while kingfishers were freeing the caged animals.

***

Up in the sky, Nuurul's flock took formation, their silhouettes sweeping over the jungle. The sight was mesmerising and everyone for miles around could see them. The world was bound to hear about today's events if they had not already.

Nuurul called out to her team. "Keep a sharp eye on any movement below and alert me of anything unusual," the queen screeched.

Chapter 28

The Ambush Part 2

Maggie and the others remained hidden as they surveyed the scene from the shadows. Maggie knew security had tightened since her last visit.

"The elephants need to make the first move," she said, knowing this would push any worker back, giving them time to reach the cages and free their friends.

A distant thud echoed, followed by a steady rhythm of trees falling. The leaves were shaking all around them as the elephant herd ran beneath them at full speed towards the worksite. Maggie's heart was pounding in her chest. She was eager to get going.

As the elephants trampled down the fences surrounding the worksite, the matriarch elephant split her herd in two, sending half toward the waterway, clearing a path to the caged animals, while the others advanced on the machinery. They trumpeted loudly as they crushed everything in their way.

Panic rippled through the workers as they frantically leaped onto boats in a bid to escape the chaos.

Azrul and the kingfishers darted down to the ground, skilfully breaking open the cages, leaving the captives to stumble out one by one.

Suddenly, a deafening bang shattered the air as smoke billowed from a nearby clearing. The proboscises and lemurs bolted back up into the treetops.

"Everyone who is at the worksite, listen carefully!" Maggie shouted. "The workers set traps throughout the site. Please watch yourselves and be careful."

Maggie spotted Azrul through the white cloudy smoke, hard at work freeing the animals from their cages. Admiration flared in Maggie's chest as she watched his bravery. She was still hoping to see Drew's family swing by. The situation around them was spiralling out of control. Animals were scattering in every direction, the fire and smoke driving them into a frenzy.

The matriarch shuffled by, heading to the waterway. Maggie swung down to her side.

"I need you to trumpet as loudly as you can and get everyone's attention," Maggie demanded, eyes fixed firmly on the elephant's gaze. "We need order, or we risk losing them all to the fire and the workers."

The matriarch raised her trunk, releasing a powerful blast that cut through the chaos like thunder. They all turned their eyes to her.

"You all need to follow me to safety!" she bellowed with a commanding and steady voice.

The animals fell into line as she led them away from the worksite and deep into the jungle. Away from the smoke, fire and traps.

Maggie saw three elephants keeping boats from being used. She swung down to them.

"Would you be able to put the fire out?" she asked, pointing at the fiery field.

Without hesitation, they sprayed the flames with their trunks, dousing the area in a torrent of water.

"That's it," Azrul growled as he appeared beside Maggie. "All the animals from the worksite are free and heading to safety."

Relief washed over Maggie, but worry continued tightening her chest. "Have you seen Drew's family?"

Azrul's expression softened. "I am afraid not. They must have been taken to the boats on the river."

***

Desperately searching for some news, Maggie radioed her sky team. “Nuurul, can you hear me?”

After a moment of static, a high-pitched voice replied, “Yes, little human. What do you need?”

Maggie kept her tone steady, fighting frustration against the queen stork’s pretentious tone. “We need to search for the captured orangutan family and any other animals who might be already on board the ships heading out to sea.”

“Ah, little Drew’s family,” Nuurul replied with a hint of disdain.

Maggie held her patience.

“Yes. They were not found at the worksite. Azrul thinks they must have been taken to the boats.”

“I have dispatched my best scouts. They will not return until they find them,” Nuurul replied.

Maggie let out a sigh of relief. Her heart lifted as she exchanged a hopeful glance with Drew and Azrul.

JOLLY ROGER

Chapter 29

A Long Journey Begins

The ambush was over. Maggie clung to her parents, her fingers tight on their shirts as relief and devastation swirled around them.

Drew's family was helped off the barge that Dhia's team had turned back from the open seas, guided in by Nuurul's watchful flock as Nabau towed it back up the river to the village. Families stumbled toward each other, breaking into tearful smiles as they embraced lost loved ones.

Maggie's thoughts drifted past the reunions to the inland quarries where the true damage lay. Her jungle, once so vibrant, was now scarred beneath the canopy. Ancient trees had fallen, and wildlife had been scattered, their habitat torn apart.

In her parents' arms, Maggie felt the weight of what was left to do. The slow, careful work of replanting, healing and restoring. The jungle could be saved, but it would take time and patience. The journey back to a balanced ecosystem was only beginning.

"Do you see it now, little girl?" a familiar hypnotic voice asked her.

Maggie turned around but could not see her friend Nabau.

"Our minds are connected. We can hear each other's thoughts. You are one of a kind, little Maggie. With some training, discipline, and persistence, you will hone your new position as saviour and be able to do good for our home planet."

Maggie smiled nervously and thought.

"What can we do about all this destruction? How will we renew the original Borneo lifestyle and way of life?"

"The animals will look to the Jungle Lords for answers. Take your time, breathe in and trust your instincts, my dear girl. Together, you will change the world as we know it. Do not forget, you have wonderful parents who believe in you and have skills of their own." With that said, Nabau's thoughts disappeared amidst the dense jungle sounds.

***

Maggie and her parents went back to their Bamboo Nest in the jungle treetops overlooking their beautiful lagoon. They all needed a well-deserved rest. Drew and his family joined up with Rango and his troop in the fruit fields for another fruit bonanza with the other jungle primates. Nuurul flew back to her sanctuary with her flock of storks, happy to be away from the dangers of the human world.

Maggie was exhausted from her lack of sleep. She knew something had to be done to clear up the now abandoned quarries, and she was going to need help both from humans and the jungle animals. Her Mama helped her map out the quarry locations with her political friends' guidance. They brought in local associations to manage the preservation of the Bornean biodiversity and its local inhabitants which were the heart of Borneo.

Soon after, Maggie and the Jungle Lords brought the Bornean locals together to restore their beautiful island as one loving and cohabiting family.

Mama's friends had been busy. Quarries had been cleared up, local farmers had been provided with land and tools to grow food for the people, and jungle animals now had space to thrive without the fear of being persecuted or kidnapped.

It was time to leave the island behind. Maggie felt sad but hopeful. She knew the Legendary Nabau would look over the Jungle Lords.

Epilogue

An Unexpected Letter

Maggie stared distantly through her bedroom window into the dense greenery of the trees, reminiscing over the bonds she had knitted throughout this jungle. She grabbed her rucksack's strap with one hand and gripped the zip tightly as she pulled it shut. As she turned away from the window, she brought her heavy rucksack up onto her thigh before swinging it up onto her shoulders. Knocking the bedside table to the ground with a crash.

As she leaned down to pick it up, a shimmer caught her eye. A lovely handwoven necklace lay there just under the windowsill. She gently lifted it up and brought it level with her eyes, letting the sunlight glimmer around it. As she did so, a warm breeze twirled around her from head to toe. The soothing warmth engulfed her entire body, and a deep murmur could be heard.

"Accept thy gift to let our minds and souls connect for evermore," Nabau's deep smooth hiss infiltrated Maggie's thoughts as she held the necklace in her cupped hand.

The warm feeling vanished as quickly as it had appeared, but the connection to her legendary friend was all so real. She looked at the necklace closely, her eyes widening when she realised the tooth hanging from the necklace was in fact a snake's fang. The sheer size of it could only mean it belonged to Nabau.

"Maggie dear, a letter has arrived for you," her Mama called out from the kitchen, snapping Maggie out of her trance and back to the Bamboo Nest and her imminent departure.

Maggie joined her parents in the kitchen, to find them just as mesmerised as she was to receive a handwritten letter. The envelope was satin maroon with gold embroidery in its corners.

"Who is it from?" Maggie asked, perplexed by the idea of receiving a letter here amidst the dense jungle.

"Open it up and let's see," Papa said, intrigued, handing it over to Maggie.

Maggie carefully sliced the letter open using her butter knife and read it out loud for the three of them to hear.

Sir Lo San Ho
NimjaCollection Ltd.
Planet Earth
To Maggie & her loving parents
The Bamboo Nest,
East Kalimantan, Borneo
Greetings fellow explorers,

I write to you in great admiration, as I am but a humble wonderer of our home, planet Earth. I thank you and congratulate you on your efforts and success in your latest Borneo endeavour.

As I sat on my balcony, watching snowflakes slowly glide with the mountain breeze, I heard a whisper of a young girl's exploits as she united an unconventional team of wild animals. The stories of jungle animals uniting to save their home against the mega corporations went viral. I was beaming with wonder when I heard a young girl was at the helm of such an adventure.

I knew in that moment I had to reach out to you no matter the cost. I hope your bravery and resolve are up for the task ahead. Your talents and skills are needed around the world. I am ready to fund your family's worldly expeditions so long as your goals align with my own. Which is to return ecosystems to their natural balance of pristine ecosystems.

I humbly request you set sail for India to make port in Kolkata, where a train will take you to the world's largest and highest natural barrier, the Himalayan Mountain range.

Your special set of skills are needed to help save the locals from certain demise and for you to perhaps discover the secrets hidden throughout the icy peaks.

If you accept this mission, please sign the bottom of this letter and hand it over to the young gentleman waiting for you by your exploration vessel, The Jolly Roger, tomorrow at noon.

Yours sincerely,
Sir Lo San Hao

Please write a review

Authors love hearing from their readers

Share your adventure! Let Nicolas know what your journey was like reading the book by leaving a fun review on your favourite online store. It will help other parents and children find the story.

(If you're under 13, ask a grown-up to help you.)

TOP TIP: be sure not to give away any of the story's secrets!

About the author

Born in bustling London and raised in the magical heart of the French Alps, Nicolas grew up with a wild imagination that only writing could bring to life.

Years later, life took him on a new kind of adventure with his wife, Jasmin, and their little explorer, Magalie. It was during their family travels that an idea began to bloom. As they trudged through snowy trails and marvelled at the vibrant greens of wild forests, the stories of brave Maggie exploring the world came to life. Sparking what has now become a beloved book series for all to enjoy.

Become a Frequent Reader

As Maggie's Adventures grow, don't miss a single exciting chapter. Be the first to know when a new book hits the shelves or when Maggie's latest adventure is ready at your favourite bookstore.

Whether you're a young reader eager for the next journey, a parent sharing stories at bedtime, a teacher inspiring curious minds or a bookseller stocking tales of wonder, Maggie's adventures are always just around the corner.

For my youngest readers, please ask your parents for consent before providing any information.

Printed in Poland
by Amazon Fulfillment
Poland Sp. z o.o., Wrocław

48352305R00093